D1316171

FOR ALL *YOU* HAVE LEFT

a novel by

Laura Miller

This book is a work of fiction. Names, characters, businesses, places and incidents are the product of the author's imagination or are used fictitiously. Any resemblance to actual events, locals or persons, living or dead, is coincidental.

Copyright © 2014 by Laura Miller.

LauraMillerBooks.com

All rights reserved. Except as permitted under the U.S. Copyright Act of 1976, no part of this publication may be reproduced, distributed or transmitted in any form or by any means or stored in a database or retrieval system.

ISBN-13: 978-1492176282
ISBN-10: 1492176281

Printed in the United States of America.

Cover design by Laura Miller.
Cover photo © *prochkailo*/Fotolia.
Title page photo © *prochkailo*/Fotolia.
Author photo © Marc Mayes.

To the Restorer of Hope
For all you have given
For all you have taken away
For all you have left

CONTENTS

For All *You* Have Left

a novel

LAURA MILLER

Man...cannot learn to forget, but hangs on the past: however far or fast he runs, that chain runs with him.

~Friedrich Nietzsche

Prologue

Only two things about that afternoon stick out to me—two things that I don't think I'll ever forget. One of those things is the smell the tires made after they had laid a jagged line of black rubber across the faded highway and into the ditch. There were tall wild flowers growing up every which way around me, but all I could think about was that bitter smell of burnt rubber. I remember a breath and then a moment where I think my mind was trying to catch up with my body. Then, there were muffled sounds and blurry images and panicked movements. But that smell was so distinct. Even now, just the thought of rubber pressed deep into a surface makes my stomach turn.

That's one thing I remember about my last ride—about the day that changed my story forever. It's the dark thing—the memory I wish I had lost, along with most of the others.

The other thing I remember, though, is my light—my little piece of hope when all hope seemed lost. I remember the way it felt in my hand. It was hard, and its edges were just sharp enough that I could almost feel pain again when I squeezed my fingers around it. I wanted that so badly—pain. I wanted to feel pain on my skin and in my bones, anywhere that wasn't my heart. I was starting to feel numb, and it was almost more terrifying than the thought of a tomorrow—a new day where I would be living someone else's life.

No one had told me at the time, but I already knew. I already knew my life was going to be different. I knew my life had changed. I remember squeezing my bloody fingers around the metal edges of that shiny figure, pressing the sharpest edge into my thumb—until I felt something. I knew I was leaving my life out there along that quiet highway, among the swaying wild flowers and that bitter smell of burnt rubber. And as the doors shut and the ambulance pulled away, my eyes fell heavy on the hope in my hand. And I remember thinking: *If I could still feel, maybe I wouldn't just wither away—maybe there was still hope for me.*

Chapter One

Four Years Earlier

"Why do you need that anyway?"

His chocolate-colored eyes find mine.

"You'll see."

I watch him go back to carefully examining the rocks scattered in the dirt and the grass. Out here, there are plenty of rocks, just like there is plenty of black dirt mixed with red clay and tall grass and some trees and nothing much else. Andrew and I are standing under a big, old oak tree on the edge of my grandpa's farm. Toward the end of one of the tree's thick branches, there's a worn-in tire swing. It catches my eye as it sways back and forth now in the soft breeze. I live just up the road. We have a dog named Buster and a cat named

Nugget, and there's an old plow contraption that my mom uses as decoration in her flower garden, but besides my grandpa's old place, the dog, the cat and the plow are as close as I ever came to growing up on a farm. My grandpa's farm isn't much today—just an old barn, some pastureland and a few cows. My dad left the farm in its heyday when he was eighteen. The story goes that he followed my mom to a little college town west of here and never looked back—well, not for at least a decade anyway. My sister and I were born in that little college town, and we called it home until my dad got a promotion and moved us here. Though, I'm pretty sure even without my dad's new job, we would have eventually made it back here anyway. My mom grew up here too, in a little brick house that's now a daycare center inside the city limits. They always talked about this place when I was younger—as if it were heaven on earth or something. From what I gather, it's not as small as it used to be. In fact, it's larger than the town I was born in, but you would never know it from just a few miles past the last stoplight—where I spent the last nine years of my life. I hated it for a while after we moved here. I hated the mosquitoes and the bees and the smell of cows that drifted our way when the wind blew just right. And most of all, I hated the fact that I couldn't just ride my bike to the ice cream shop or to the movies. In fact, I hated this place pretty much up until about the time that Andrew Amsel first kissed me.

"I need a sharp one."

Andrew's talking to me, but it really sounds as if it's only to himself. I furrow my eyebrows and shake my head. I'm used to his little breaks from ordinary, everyday life, like his little paper-airplane notes that sometimes fly into the classroom from the hall and land near my desk or the groundhog trap he made in shop class—not to actually catch the groundhog that had been burrowing holes into the school's lawn since March and not even just to have an excuse to get out of class and check it throughout the day. No, the day he built it, he came up to me at my locker with a proud smile on his face and whispered into my ear: "I found a way to see you every day. Look outside the window during English class." And sure enough, later that same day, I dropped my English book onto a desk, sat down and looked out the window, and there he was, fiddling with a wooden box and smiling back at me. It was just another ordinary day with Andrew Amsel.

Andrew's house is across the road and two houses down from mine. I first learned this about nine years ago, before I knew anything about mascara or eyeliner and when high school seemed only like some distant dream. It was the same day we moved here actually. It was raining. I remember that because it seemed fitting. My life already sucked because I had no friends; I had just left them all in Independence. I figured: *Why shouldn't the weather suck here too?* But it was only a couple hours maybe after the last box had been unloaded from the truck that two little boys showed up at our front door. I remember the clouds were just starting to float away when the taller boy asked if my sister and I wanted to play Wiffle ball. I hated Wiffle ball, and I didn't so much care for boys, but I would have done anything, I think, to get out of unpacking for a while. Unpacking was right up there with no friends and the sucky weather.

"Found one!"

My thoughts are instantly broken as Andrew takes my hand and gently pulls me to the tree's trunk and plants his feet right in front of it.

"You put it in a tree, it's forever," he says, looking at me with his big, brown eyes.

I feel him squeeze my hand before he puts the sharp edge of the rock to the tree's bark and starts carving. After a couple moments, he has a big *A* etched into the surface of the tree. I continue to watch his hand and the rock in it as he draws a plus sign followed by a big *L*. Then, he traces over the letters a few more times.

"Now it's forever," I say.

"Just about." He sends me a quick glance before going back to his carving.

My eyes follow his movements as he puts the rock to the bark yet again, but this time, I can't see what he's etching into the tree. He's at it for a good while, but I don't mind just watching him and the way his forearm muscles move with the turn of the rock in his hand. His arms aren't huge—not like the guys who spend every evening in the school's weight room, lifting and grunting and trying to outdo each other. Andrew's arms are just right. They're strong enough to throw a ball across a baseball diamond, tough enough to lift the heavy things I can't and sturdy enough to scoop me up into his arms at just the right times.

"There!"

He moves away from his carving and stands beside the tree's trunk.

I reread the *A + L* that now has a heart encircling it, and then my eyes travel to the words below it, and I feel the corners of my lips suddenly edging high up my face.

"Forever and a day," I say out loud, reading the inscription below the letters.

My eyes fall into Andrew's. I can't imagine loving someone more. He's my perfect—one part solid as a rock, one part crazy, one part starry-eyed dreamer. I could listen to him talk about the life we're going to have in the little house in the country and how happy we're going to be for hours under this old tree. I don't know how many hours we've spent doing that same thing already.

"I'm gonna marry you someday, Andrew Amsel."

Even though his face is straight, I watch his wild eyes burn with passion. I know those eyes, and I love those eyes.

"I'm gonna make you so happy," he eventually says. His voice is raspy and passionate.

He pulls me into him and then kisses me slowly and softly and deeply, almost as if he's claiming my soul for himself. And when our kiss breaks, he puts his forehead to mine and one hand to my cheek, while the other strokes my hair.

"Marry me tomorrow, Logan."

I pause, as a word dances on my lips but never leaves them.

"No, really, let's get married," he says again.

"Andrew." I start to laugh. "We're still in high school. We can't get married."

"Why not? We're both eighteen; there's no law against it."

My smile widens. "That has to be a bad idea." I think I'm more so trying to convince myself just how bad of an idea it really is.

"There is nothing either good or bad, but thinking makes it so." He recites the lines straight from Shakespeare himself.

I shake my head. For some reason, of all the lines and quotes he's ever heard or read, that one is the one that stuck. I think I hear it at least every other day.

"I love you, Andrew, but I can't marry you in high school."

He pushes his lips out and to one side and narrows one eye. He doesn't seem satisfied.

"We'd spend our honeymoon grounded, doing chemistry homework," I say.

He dramatically inhales and then slowly forces the breath out. "Good point."

I laugh, and then he gently pulls me down to the ground until we're resting on the grass and our backs are up against the old tree.

"I love you so much, Logan."

He sets the rock down onto the ground, and I quickly recover it and then let my head fall into his lap—just like I have done nearly a million times before. There are cicadas in the trees around us, and they're singing their summer song in unison. And pushing over us, trying desperately to warm our shade, is a soft, steady stream of air.

I feel Andrew pick up a strand of my long hair and then gently lay it back down again. He does this over and over again. It makes me feel safe somehow.

"Are you happy, Andrew?"

A silent moment passes between us. Then, I hear his soft, thoughtful voice.

"It's just another day with you—the best day of my life."

I nuzzle my cheek against his leg and press against my heart the rock that just penned our love into the wood of eternity.

"And someday," he goes on, "we're gonna get married, and I'm gonna make sure you know I love you every day—whether I'm by your side or not, you're gonna know I love you. I'll probably drive ya crazy making sure you know, but at least you'll be a loved crazy person."

He pauses, and I snicker a little.

"We'll fight, probably," he continues, in a way that seems as if he's just now come to that conclusion. "And you're gonna pout in your corner, and I'm gonna pout in mine. And we're gonna pout until we just can't hide how much we love each other anymore, and then I'm gonna kiss you so hard. And then we're gonna promise each other that we'll never fight again. And then we're gonna grow old together, and I'm still gonna love you."

He stops then, but he keeps stroking my hair.

"I'm gonna love you, Logan, forever and a day," he whispers.

I don't say anything because I know he's in his own, little world now, dreaming about our future. He breathes evenly, peacefully now. I can picture the little smile hanging on his lips—the little grin he saves only for times like this. It's not the same smile he wears at school. In the halls of Truman High, he wears a poker face—a perfect, little smirk that's one-part sexy and one-part mysterious. He hides his crazy there. He hides the dreams that I know are constantly in his head. He hides them so well that sometimes he even fools me into believing that lunch and the next baseball game are the only future he's ever thought about. But I guess that way no one bothers Andrew Amsel. His brother tries but to no avail. The girls love him; the guys respect him. He's cute, and he's a natural athlete, which helps a little with his tough-guy façade, I guess. But if you know Andrew Amsel like I do, you know his real strength isn't in anything you can see.

"Babe." His soft whisper instantly halts my thoughts.

"Hmm?" I angle my face up toward his.

"Two or three?"

I think about it for a second.

"Three," I say.

He pauses.

"Dog or cat?"

"Dog," I say.

He nods in satisfaction. And I rest my head in his lap again as he goes back to his dreams and to picking up the pieces of my hair and then laying them back down again.

"Three scraggly kids and a dog," he confirms.

I can hear the smile in his voice—even over the cicadas' song, and it makes my heart dance because I see what he sees too. I see the little house in the country—the row of apple trees, the purple and orange wildflowers swaying in the breeze, even the dog. I see it all, all from the view of some old porch swing somewhere. I know it sounds crazy, but minus one detail—one pesky, little detail that's still a little blurry—I see it all so clearly—almost as if it were a snapshot right out of our future.

I nuzzle my cheek against Andrew's leg again and let go of a happy sigh. Crazy or not, somehow I just know that from that old porch swing, I can see the stuff my dreams are made of.

Chapter Two

Last Day

"This is the last kiss that I'm ever gonna give you—at this locker," Andrew announces.

I look up at him. He's wearing a wide grin.

"Well, you better make it a good one then," I say.

His grin quickly turns mischievous, and he doesn't even bother looking around to see who's watching. He just touches one hand to the back of my neck and the other to the small of my back, and he leans in. I close my eyes and instantly feel his shallow breaths on my lips. It feels raw and unscripted as he moves his tender lips over mine. And then he slips his tongue into my mouth, leans farther into me and kisses me harder. He plays with my tongue, and I kiss him back as my stomach does a somersault. And after a few more exhilarating moments of his breaths and his lips and his tongue, his kiss breaks from my lips, and he presses his forehead against mine.

"How was that?" he whispers.

I feel my lips start to edge up my face and into a wide smile. It's his answer, and he knows it.

"I love you so much, Logan," he whispers into my ear.

Then, before I can say anything, he slaps my butt and walks away.

"Get a room," I hear a boy from across the hall yell out to Andrew.

Andrew doesn't even bother to look back. "That's a great idea," he says, right before he disappears down another hallway. "Maybe I can use yours."

Andrew's voice trails off, and my attention goes to the boy. He looks defeated, but when he finds my gaze, his face brightens.

"Hi, Logan."

"Hi, James."

"You still coming to our house before graduation?" he asks.

I nod my head. "Mm hmm."

He flashes me a content smile and then continues his trek down the hallway. "I'll see you later then," he says.

I laugh quietly to myself and turn back toward my locker. There's only one textbook and a notebook on the shelf. I grab them both and go to close the locker before I stop and spot a note taped to the inside of the door.

I quickly peel the folded piece of paper off and fall back against the locker door. It latches shut with a click as I press the books against my chest and open the note with both hands. And instantly, my eyes go to reading the familiar handwriting:

Logan,

I can't believe we walk down that aisle in a cap and gown together tonight. I really wish it was a church and you were in a different kind of white dress, but I can wait, I guess. But not too long, okay?

Logan, if I haven't told you today yet that I love you, find me and kick my ass. Because Logan, I've loved you ever since that rainy afternoon I showed up at your door. And I loved you that Monday too when you were that scared, little new girl in the third grade. I wanted to take your hand then and tell you that I'd walk with you for the rest of my life—that I'd hold your hand, so you'd never have to walk alone, so you'd never have to be scared. And the only reason I didn't is because Doug Sorenson said you had some kind of reptile (yeah, reptile) disease and that if I even went near you that I'd die in three seconds flat.

Reptile disease? I laugh to myself, then continue reading:

And, yeah, I believed him until he made you that dumb Valentine's card the next year and stuck all those lame hearts all over it. Damn Sorenson. Anyway, Logan, the point here is that I love you. I love you forever and a day. Happy graduation day!

P.S. You're still coming with me to Jenson slab afterward, right?

P.P.S. You look as sexy as hell in those shorts. I'm really happy that no one gives a shit about dress code today!

Love,
Andrew

I take in a deep breath and let out a happy grin as I refold the note and slide it into the back pocket of my jean shorts. The ring of the first bell makes me jump, but before I can start my hike to my last class, I catch the number on the locker right next to mine. It's his locker. The number on the little, metal door is *92*—our anniversary. We don't really have a real date—a date when we first started going out or dating or whatever. I guess because we just kind of always were. Andrew picked the day we would use though. It's the first day we ever had lunch together—September 2—in a little cafeteria at Cedar Elementary. He says I traded him my milk for his cookie. I don't remember the trade, and I have no idea how he remembers the exact date—I barely remember it was even September when I moved here—but he swears he does.

I pull my books closer to my chest. God, sometimes I still can't believe I fell for that messy-haired little boy with the plastic Wiffle ball bat slung across his shoulders. But more so, I guess, I can't believe just how much I love him because in the end, I absolutely love that crazy boy with everything I am.

Chapter Three

Graduation Night

"**M**arry me," he whispers.

His hat and tassel are long gone, but his black gown is still draped around his body.

"What?"

I keep my eyes planted in the black sky and the sea of stars as I lace my fingers in his and make myself comfortable against the metal grooves of the truck bed.

"Marry me," he says again.

I don't say anything. I just smile. And out of the corner of my eye, I watch him turn over onto his side and play with the quilt beneath us.

"Logan, remember when we were kids, and I always used to say that even if you were the last girl in the world, I'd never marry you?"

I laugh softly.

"Yeah," I say, meeting his eyes.

"Logan, I said it, but..."

He pauses, then reaches behind him and pulls out from the darkness a little journal and holds it out to me.

I stare at it for a second before I slowly reach for it. The journal is small, and its edges are worn away, and down the front of its soft, leather cover in big, block letters are the words: *KEEP OUT OR DIE!*

My eyes dart to his. "Andrew, I don't have a death wish."

He rolls his eyes and sighs playfully.

"It was for the little brother. It worked...I think."

I watch his gaze wander off as he seems to get stuck on a thought. Then, all of a sudden, his eyes snap back to me.

"Go ahead," he says, gesturing toward the book.

He's wearing a boyish grin. I keep my stare in his for a second or two longer. Then, I slowly pull back the journal's faded cover and look back up at him for further instruction.

"Read." He holds his phone's light to the book.

I turn the first, blank page and then stop. I stop at the big, sloppy handwriting that scrolls crooked down the next page. There's a date at the top. It reads *September 2, 2000*. I take a second to add up the years. He was nine. We were nine.

"Andrew, is this really yours?"

I just can't bring myself to believe that Andrew Amsel kept a journal. I mean, he had his moments—those moments when I could maybe find it believable that the spirited, little boy I knew when we were nine wrote his thoughts down. But a journal?

I watch his eyelids fall over his eyes as he lowers his head.

"My mom made me keep it. Believe me, I protested. I even tried to flush the first one she gave me down the toilet."

He stops and laughs.

"I flushed it six times without it going anywhere before she caught me. And in the end, Mom won, and I remember her telling me that someday it would be fun to read it. I didn't give a shit about that back then, but now that I think about it, I guess she was talking about today—that maybe today, it would be fun to read it."

I can't help my eyes from turning suspicious.

"Go on." He gestures toward the little journal again. "Read it."

Again, I force my eyes to his little-boy words barely hanging on the page:

There's this new girl in my class. She lives down the road. Her name is Logan. It's a funny name. Anyway, she can't hit a ball. Her hair stinks like flowers, and she's too tall.

I finish reading over the words and look back up at him with pretend narrowed eyes.

"My hair stinks...like flowers?" I ask.

He laughs.

"And apparently, you could be too tall," he says.

"There's still more." He gestures with his eyes toward the bottom of the page.

I look closer. I wouldn't have noticed the tiny letters scribbled upside down along the bottom of the page if he wouldn't have pointed them out.

I turn the journal upside down and squint my eyes to see the writing:

She can hit a ball. Flowers don't smell that bad, and I wish I was as tall as her.

I peek at him through my eyelashes. I'm pretty sure there's a questioning look plastered to my face.

"I never wanted to find out what my mom would do to me if she caught me being ugly or worst yet, in a lie," he explains. "She promised she wouldn't read it, but you know my mom."

I shrug my shoulders and then nod my head in agreement. Over the years, Mrs. Amsel has become like a second mom to me, so I do know her. And I know she loves her boys, but I also know that she could never resist the temptation to learn more about them if an opportunity in the form of, say, a discarded, open journal presented itself.

"Go on, keep reading," he says.

I laugh and turn the page. It's dated the next day, *September 3, 2000*:

I told Logan today that I wouldn't marry her even if she was the last girl in the world. She's annoying, and I hate her.

I suck in a big breath but then notice the tiny letters again at the bottom of the page and quickly train my eyes to them:

I would marry her. She's not so bad, and I don't hate her. I don't hate her at all.

I look up at him again.

"It kind of goes on like that for another hundred pages or so," he says. "Every once in a while there's a rant about how much I hate the lunch ladies' beef stroganoff or how much I wish my brother was a puppy, but for the most part, it's all about you."

He stops and chuckles to himself.

"And there are no disclaimers about the stroganoff or the puppy brother either," he adds. "I wasn't lying about those things."

I shake my head and laugh before I catch his stare again. And in that short moment, his eyes seem to have turned serious all of a sudden.

"But there's one more I want you to see."

He pulls out another journal. And from what I can tell, this one isn't so tattered. Its edges aren't really worn, and it still has a bright-colored cover.

"Yeah, so it's kind of addicting," he says. "I'm still a hard-ass. Don't be fooled."

I give him a sarcastic look and then carefully take the journal from his hands.

"The last entry," he says.

I fall into his soft, brown eyes then, and my heart melts a little. I really do love this boy—even more than I did a moment ago. How is it possible to love someone so much and then to love them even more? And it's not just any love either. It's that kind of love where you know you would do anything for him, go anywhere, even take on his pain if you could—that kind of love.

I return my attention to the journal and flip to the last page with words on it. It's dated *June 5, 2009*.

My eyes quickly venture back to his.

"That's today," I say.

I watch him slowly nod his head before I find the words on the page again and follow over them:

I've known this girl Logan for nine, miserable years now. Her eyes are too green. Her smile is all wrong. I wouldn't marry her if she were the last girl in the world. And she still can't hit a ball.

I playfully narrow my eyes at him before I catch the tiny letters again at the bottom of the page:

I've known this girl Logan for nine, happy years now. Her eyes are beautiful. Her smile is perfect. I would marry her every day of my life if I could. And she can still hit a ball—better than I can.

I can feel my heart breaking into a million, little pieces as I follow over his tiny words at the bottom of the page one more time. And I think it's those same, tiny words that remind me that he's no longer the little boy I shared a childhood with.

"I know in my heart that you're the one," Andrew whispers low and near my ear.

His words are breathy and passionate. And instead of seeing his perfect, boyish grin when I look up, I catch a box. And inside the box is a ring. And above the ring are two longing eyes.

"I know I'm going to spend the rest of my life with you. Please, marry me, Logan Ada Cross."

I search his eyes for a moment, but only for a moment. That's all the time I need.

"Okay," I whisper.

"Wednesday," he adds, with a hopeful plea in his dark brown eyes.

I press my lips together, until I just can't hold back a smile any longer.

"Okay," I whisper.

Chapter Four

Bells

"Logan."

I open my eyes to a shadowy figure hovering over me, blocking out the sun.

"You look beautiful." Andrew leans down and kisses me on the cheek.

I smile and sit up.

"You like it," I ask. "I have another one if you don't like it."

He shakes his head. "I love it."

My stomach fills with butterflies. I'm glad he likes it. After four long days of deciding what to wear today, I came to the conclusion that this one was the one; this one was perfect. It's simple—no lace, no crazy cut-outs, just a simple, white sundress. I would have been crushed if he had showed even the slightest sign that he didn't like it. I wanted to look perfect today. I wanted to look perfect for him.

"The dress is new, and the earrings are my mom's, so they're old." I pull on one of the earrings. "And these shoes are Hannah's." I point to the little, white boat shoes on my feet. "She won't miss them—today anyway." I send Andrew a mischievous grin, but then it slowly fades. "But I don't have anything blue."

Andrew stares at me for a second, then falls into the hammock beside me, puts his elbows on his knees and his fists under his chin and just sits there quietly.

"I got it," he says, after another second. And I watch him pull his baseball state championship ring off his finger. "It's blue."

He takes my hand and slides the ring onto my thumb. There's a spark in his eyes. He looks so happy.

I hold my hand out in front of me and fixate on the dancing sparkles in the blue jewel.

"It's perfect," I say, as I look up at Andrew. And for some reason, it's as if I were looking at him for the first time because I notice him—like really notice him—as being a man and not just a boy. He's wearing dark slacks, a light blue collared shirt and a gray vest with his black motorcycle boots. It just might be the most dressed up I've ever seen him.

"You look really good," I say.

He looks down at himself.

"You think so?"

It's cute the way he seems so unsure of himself all of a sudden. I rarely see this side of him.

"Mm hmm," I say, nodding my head. "You look perfect...ly sexy."

He flashes me a wide grin.

"Now, save that thought for later, my dear," he says, giving me a wink.

His confidence is back now.

I laugh softly and try to smooth the wrinkles, which the little eyelets in the hammock made, out of my dress.

"I don't think you're supposed to see me before," I say. "It's bad luck."

Not even a second goes by before I feel the tip of Andrew's finger touch my chin and then start to lift my face.

"Who believes in luck?" I watch his lips light up his handsome features. "You?" he asks.

I shake my head.

"Me neither," he says.

I start to smile too, but then it slowly fades.

"Andrew."

His soft eyes catch mine.

"When we get married, you'll still love me like you do now, right?" I lower my eyes. "It won't change us, right?"

I peek through my eyelashes and notice Andrew's face turning serious—not scared or anything—just as if he had thought about it too maybe.

"It more than likely won't change you," he says.

My gaze quickly darts up toward his again.

"But you?" I ask it as if I'm scared to hear his answer.

He nods his head.

"You'll change me all right, Logan."

I stare at him with questioning eyes. I don't want him to change, and I sure don't want to be the reason he changes.

"You'll make me a better man," he says, before I can say anything.

I suck in a deep breath and command my heart to beat again. I love him so much. It scares me sometimes when I think about how lucky...blessed...I am to have found the love of my life the first time around. I never had to cry the tears that my best friend Sara had to when she broke up with her first boyfriend our sophomore year. And I never had to experience the indecision or the *what ifs* that my sister Hannah talked about every time she climbed into my bed and said she just needed me to listen. There was always some boy whom she wanted to date and always another one whom she had second thoughts about letting go. I got them all confused, but like I said, it didn't matter; I just needed to listen. But I did always wish that Sara and Hannah could have found someone like Andrew when they were nine too. Then, maybe they could have saved some of their tears. Life was a whole lot less dramatic for me. I liked it that way. But more than I loved a simple existence, I loved Andrew Amsel.

"You ready to get married?"

I force my eyes to his.

"More than ready," I say.

He stands up and holds out his hand. I rest mine—the one with the little diamond on my ring finger and the big blue jewel on my thumb—in his. He helps me to my feet, and we start off toward his bike in the driveway. But we only get a few yards before I hear his soft voice again.

"You tell your parents?"

I feel my lips instinctively push to one side as I shake my head.

He doesn't say anything; he doesn't ask why. He already knows why.

"You?" I ask.

"Nah."

I slowly nod my head. I already knew his answer too. And it's not that I didn't want to tell my parents. I did. I really did. And it's not that they don't love Andrew because they do. And it's not even that I don't think they would understand because they will. My mom and my dad got married when they were eighteen too. And they were nineteen when they had Hannah. My mom was a freshman in college, but after she had Hannah, she never went back to school. I think that everyone might have that one *what if* in their life, and I think a college degree is my mom's. And I know she wants that for Hannah and me. I know she wants us to become teachers or doctors or something like that. And I wish I could tell her that I can still do something like that—get some degree that will make both of my parents happy—*and* be married to Andrew and have them believe me, but I know they've got good reason not to. That's why I didn't tell them though. And I'd ask Andrew why he didn't tell his parents, but I already know the *why* to that too. He was afraid they'd tell mine.

"You still want to do this?" His voice is timid and almost broken.

I immediately stop walking and narrow in on his face. He's looking at me through hooded eyes now. And even though I can't tell if he looks more nervous or sad, I just want to comfort him.

"Andrew, I love you so much. I just can't wait another day. And plus, I imagined myself probably a million times in the last few days standing with you in front of that judge in this dress on this exact day. It already feels so real; I can't even imagine not actually living it."

I make sure to look deep into his soft, brown eyes. "I want to spend forever with you, Andrew."

A moment passes between us in silence before I instinctively squeeze his hand.

"Wait, you're not having second thoughts, are you?" I ask.

Andrew looks down at the ground and then back up at me. There's a second where I think I might have stopped breathing, but then I spot a soft, sexy grin returning to his face.

"You're kidding, right?" he asks. "If it weren't for parents and high school and a dumb, unspoken rule that says you have to be a certain age to marry the girl you've loved since you were a kid, I would have already married you, Logan. You know that."

I let go of a thankful breath as I rest my head on his arm and start walking again. I do—know that.

"I just don't want you to have any regrets, that's all," he adds, kissing my forehead.

I lift my eyes to his again because I know what he's not saying. He doesn't have to say that he worries I'll regret not telling my parents. And he doesn't have to tell me that he worries how I would feel if they disowned me or us if we go through with this today. He doesn't have to say any of it because I can read it all on his face.

"Andrew, my parents love you. And they know how much I love you. And they'll still love us both after today too. I know that."

I stop walking and rest a hand on either side of his face. "And I'm marrying you today no matter what. Nothing else matters. Nothing else means more to me. I promise you that anything that I could ever regret about today will never mean more to me than you."

I lower my hands and shrug my shoulders.

"So, the way I see it, the worse thing that comes out of today is having to decide who gets to drive the Hoveround when we're eighty."

Andrew holds a long, fixed look on me. I can tell he wants to smile, but he's not quite sure yet.

"You know I get to drive it, right?" he asks.

"Who says?"

"The mailbox you drove my bike into last weekend."

"I scuffed it," I correct him. "I scuffed the mailbox, and there wasn't even a scratch on the bike. And if you wouldn't have been distracting me with all that gears and clutch mumbo jumbo, I would have had it all under control."

There's a second where he's glaring at me with his mischievous boy-grin, then in the next second, he scoops me into his arms, and I feel a high-pitched squeal push past my lips.

"Babe, all that gears and clutch mumbo jumbo was what you needed to actually drive the bike," he says, laughing softly into my ear.

I flash him a confident glance. "Well, maybe you should have been telling me more about the brakes mumbo jumbo, sweetie."

He slowly nods his head. "Touché," he says, before planting a wet kiss on my lips. And soon, a grin returns to his face. "Well, babe, you look as sexy as hell behind the handlebars of my bike." He sets me down onto the part of the leather behind the driver's seat and swings his leg over the bike. "But you look even sexier behind me behind the bars."

There's a smirk on my face now; I can feel it.

"Sexier and a whole lot safer, you mean?"

"Exactly," he says, handing me the pink helmet he bought for me the day he got his motorcycle license

27

almost a year ago. "Sexier and a whole lot safer," he confirms.

I squeeze the helmet on over my thick hair, and then he hands me a backpack, and I throw that on too. And after he kicks up the kickstand and starts the bike, he twists around and catches my gaze.

"Now, let's go get married," he says.

"Give me your hand."

He looks at me for a moment and smiles, then holds out his left hand.

I position my hand on top of his and snap a photo of the new rings resting at the bottom of our ring fingers.

"Are you happy, Logan?" he asks me after I lower the camera from my face.

I look up at him.

"It's just another day with you—the best day of my life," I say.

He searches my eyes for a moment, then kisses the top of my forehead and presses his lips hard against mine. And when our kiss breaks, he smiles at me. And it's not just any smile. It's his smile—that one that holds a lifetime of promises that I know he won't break, that one that says: *I'll never leave you. I'll never let you go. I'm here forever. I love you.* I love that smile.

"You ready?" he asks.

I nod my head, and he lifts me up and sets me onto the little backseat. Then, he swings his leg over the bike and straddles it, while I make sure my sundress is positioned just right.

"You know they're going to kill us," I whisper into his ear, as I hand him the camera.

He's quiet for a moment—but only for a moment.

"Babe, if I die tomorrow, I die a happy man—with your ring on my finger."

He reaches back and squeezes my leg.

"Your helmet, Wife." He hands me the pink helmet.

"Thank you, Husband."

I take the helmet and squeeze it over my head.

"Husband," I say again, just to feel it on my tongue.

I hear the click of the helmet's strap under my chin and watch as Andrew slides the marriage license and the camera inside the backpack and zips it closed.

"Guard this with your life," he says, angling back toward me.

I force my arms through the bag until it's resting on my back.

"Oh, and I put my sweatshirt in there too just in case you get cold on the way back," he says. "Let me know if we need to stop, so you can put it on."

I nod my head, and the big, pink helmet moves with it.

"I love you, Logan Amsel. Forever and a day." He reaches back and squeezes my leg again.

I adjust the backpack, then tighten my arms around his waist.

"I love you too, Andrew Amsel."

There's a moment, and then suddenly, the purr of the bike's engine fills the air around us. The sound grows louder and louder as the bike leaves the curb in one swift motion, forcing my body backward. I squeeze my arms tighter around Andrew's waist.

"Forever and a day," I whisper, pressing my cheek against his shoulder as the warm June air brushes feverishly over the parts of my bare skin.

Chapter Five

Four Years Later

(The Present)

"This is a nice place you got here, sis," Hannah says, throwing herself onto the couch. "It's different now that it's finally all decorated—homier, I think."

I pull out a glass from the cabinet. "You want some tea?"

Her face darts toward mine in a severe kind of way. "You never have to ask, you know?"

I laugh and grab the tea from the fridge and pour two glasses as Hannah goes on another tangent.

"I'm just so happy you've got your own place. And this one is so much better than your last one. And much, much better than the one before that."

I look up at her.

"Hannah, the one before that was my dorm room."

"I know. That one stunk...literally."

I chuckle and shake my head. "It did," I agree.

"Your own place. No roommates. A great, big-girl job. I just feel like you're so grown up," she says and then stops.

"It's like you're not Little Logan anymore."

If looks could kill, I'm pretty sure Hannah would be laid out on the couch by now. I really don't even mean to send her my death stare; it just comes naturally.

Hannah eventually looks up and scrunches her lips to one side.

"I'm sorry, I mean Ada...Lada."

She finally settles on the nickname she made up for me that I've also come to answer to.

Having a sister definitely comes with its advantages. But being so comfortable that you just spit the first thing that comes to your mind out of your mouth is not one of them.

"Lada, it just came out," Hannah pleads.

I continue to stare at her across the empty space. But I guess I really can't be mad. She had called me Logan for eighteen years. I imagine it's hard to retrain your brain after almost two decades of knowing someone by a different name, and I imagine it's even harder when you have a brain the size of a pea.

"It's fine," I say, picking up the two glasses.

But I'm still trying to shake off the sound of my own name when we hear a loud thud outside the door.

I catch Hannah's face light up, and then suddenly, that look somewhere in between mischief and curiosity fills her eyes. I recognize it instantly.

She jumps up and rushes to the door as I bring our drinks to the living room and set them down onto the coffee table.

"What is it?" I ask.

She's got her face plastered to the door; her eyes are glued to the peep hole.

"I think someone's moving in across the hall."

"Oh," I say, in the most enthused voice I can muster.

I haven't had a neighbor for two weeks, and now, I think I've already kind of gotten used to it. Plus, I've only ever had weird neighbors. In the dorms in college, the girl across the hall always left messages on my door about her Renaissance club meetings. I'm not sure what I did to convince her that I would ever be the slightest bit interested in "keeping the Renaissance alive," as she put it, but that didn't stop her from stalking my door twenty-four-seven with little sticky notes that included words like: *Good morrow*, *prithee* and *fare thee well*.

Then, there was Suri. When I was nineteen, I moved off campus and right next door to Suri. Suri had a strange obsession with cats. She believed that cats were really people on their second lives. She had four of them—cats—even though I think we were only supposed to have one—and each had a story about whom he or she was in his or her first life. One was a doctor who practiced herbal remedies; one traveled with the Russian ballet; one was an aide to Ronald Reagan. The other... What was the fourth one?

"Hannah, what were Suri's cats in their past lives?"

Hannah doesn't move her eye from the peep hole. She doesn't question my query either. Both responses are expected.

"A ballerina, a doctor, a presidential aide and a TV meteorologist," she says, without skipping a beat.

"That's right," I say out loud. "The cat that could predict the weather."

How did I forget that one?

"O.M.G.," Hannah squeals. "Lada, get over here. You've got to see this."

I'm almost positive that whatever it is on the other side of my door, it doesn't warrant me running over to Hannah and shoving her out of the way, but I do it anyway—just in case Publishers Clearing House or Brad Pitt is on the other side.

"What?" I ask, forcing one eye to the peep hole.

"Is he the mover or the one moving in?" she asks.

"I don't see anything." My shoulders slump. No big check. No sexy actor.

"Just wait," she says. "He'll come back."

I stand there motionless, breathing into the little space between my lips and the door, for a few more seconds—just long enough that I start to feel as if I've somehow turned into the weird, creepy neighbor that I'm so afraid of. Then, suddenly, he walks by and disappears into the apartment across the hall. I immediately gasp, turn and quickly force my back against the door.

"It's the mover, right?" I say to Hannah.

She pushes me out of the way and glues her eye to the peep hole again.

"But he's the only one. Have you ever seen just one mover?" she asks.

I push my lips together.

"He's got a weird obsession with his mother or his cats have afterlives, right?" I ask her.

She doesn't say anything for a second.

"Or he's just as sane as his abs are perfect," she says. "And God, his eyes are so blue."

I let out an audible sigh.

"Come on, Lada," she scolds, "be excited. You don't see eyes like that every day—or abs, for that matter."

I gather myself and slowly make my way back over to the tea on the coffee table.

"Hannah, he's probably got a girlfriend or a wife or he's a priest or something."

I pick up a glass and take a drink. I think I'm trying to convince myself just as much as I'm trying to convince Hannah.

"Lada, he's no priest," she states, confidently.

I shrug my shoulders to try to show some indifference.

"But I'll look for a ring," she adds.

"Hannah," I whisper loudly. "You're being Creepy McCreepster. What if he can see your big eyeball through that hole?"

She tilts her head toward me just enough that I can see her face—the one that's pretending to be put out.

"You're kidding, right?" she asks. "He can't see me."

I flash her an impatient look. "Yeah, well, he can probably hear you."

She furrows her brow and purses her lips. She knows I'm right.

I take another sip of my tea.

I really hope there's something wrong with this guy—something that would make it easy for Hannah to just let it go—because Hannah anywhere near my love life scares the hell out of me. And I already know where this is all going.

"O.M.G.," she squeals in her high-pitched voice.

"Hannah," I scold in my loudest whisper.

She turns her head to the side and stares intensely at me. "You guys have the same tall lamp."

I close my eyes and exhale.

"Hannah, everyone who shops at Target has the same tall lamp."

She turns her face away again and goes back to her peeping. "It's a sign," I hear her whisper into the door.

I laugh and fall into the couch with my tea in hand. "A sign that he shops at Target," I mumble under my breath.

Chapter Six

Next door

It's 6:30 in the morning. I'm barely awake. The light pouring in through every window in this little apartment is blinding me. I readjust my sweatshirt and let it hang over the boxers I sleep in every night. There are exactly eleven steps from my bedroom to the door. Sometimes I get bored of doing the same thing over and over again, so I count. *Ten. Eleven.* I swing open the door and reach down to pick up my paper. It's there every morning—without fail. I slide the rubber band off—like I do every morning—and unfold its accordion pages. And as if it were second nature, I turn to the last page just when the door across the hall opens and a man freezes in the doorway and stares at me.

I panic. I feel as if I should be embarrassed of stalking him yesterday—as if he knows or something—even though it really was Hannah who was doing most of the stalking. I quickly roll the newspaper back up and force my lips to move.

"Hi," I say and quickly drop my eyes.

Oh my God. I notice my bare legs where my sweatshirt ends. It looks as if I'm not wearing any pants. I tug at the boxers, trying to will them to be longer, but I don't think they're any match against my oversized sweatshirt.

"Hi," he says, with a warm smile. "I just moved in."

There's a second where I don't say anything. I know it's my turn to talk, but I haven't got the foggiest idea of what to say. What if he heard Hannah yesterday through the door? What can I say that makes me look less like a creeper?

"Really?" I ask, at last, giving him a pretend, puzzled look. My voice sort of cracks, and I clear my throat and try my best to recover. "You must be a really quiet mover. I didn't even notice."

He chuckles and looks down at his welcome mat.

"I tried to keep it down," he says, looking back up. "I'm Jorgen."

He takes a step and extends his hand toward me.

"Ada," I say, meeting his hand.

"Ada," he repeats, almost as if he's questioning whether I know my own name or not. But he seems strangely relieved, at the same time.

My eyebrows instinctively wrinkle a little in response to his questioning look as I take my hand back and run it through my wild strands of hair. But I figure out quickly that trying to tame my bed head is pretty useless, and I give up.

He's still staring at me—as if he's trying to place me in his memory or something.

"We've uh...," I stutter. "We've never met, I don't think," I try to reassure him.

He doesn't quite look satisfied.

"I'm a...," I start and then laugh nervously. "I'm not a one-night stand or a girl you never called, I promise," I say, forcing out another laugh.

He doesn't even crack a smile, and his deep stare on me turns even more unreadable. I put my hand on my doorknob and start to turn it. I'm now completely and utterly embarrassed. But at least the mystery is solved. He's a weirdo who stares *a lot* and who can't take a joke. I can't wait to tell Hannah.

"No," he suddenly says.

I stop instantly and slowly turn back toward him. His eyes are wide now, and his face is flushed.

"That's not what I was thinking." His voice is softer this time.

"No, I know. I'm sorry. I was just kidding," I rattle off.

He lowers his eyes and shakes his head. "I know," he says, starting to grin.

Then, there's another awkward pause, and I start to turn again but something stops me. It seems as though I've come to acquire some sort of an affinity for strange neighbors. Plus, maybe the joke wasn't the best for having just met someone. I feel weird just leaving on that.

"Are you new to Columbia?" I ask because I don't know what else to say.

He looks up at me.

"Uh...no, actually, I'm just moving from across town. You?"

"No," I say, "not new. I've basically been here my whole life. My family moved here from Independence when I was young."

He nods his head. "I grew up in a small town east of here—Berger."

I immediately recognize the name. I did a story several months back about a guy in that area. The little town was next to some other small town, and they were both known for something. It takes me a second, but it finally comes to me.

"By Hermann," I say. "You have the wineries."

He nods. "That would be us."

There's a pause before I open my mouth again. "Well, welcome to this side of town. It's quiet. Nice. No complaints."

He's smiling by the time I finish.

"I like what I see so far," he says, looking around and eventually landing back on my *pantless* legs.

And that would be my cue to exit. I haven't ruled out that he's not a dangerous weirdo yet.

"Well, it was nice to meet you," I quickly stammer.

I reach again for the doorknob.

"It was nice to meet you too, Ada."

I meekly smile in his direction one last time and then turn the knob and push through my door. It closes behind me, and I twist the dead bolt and let go of a breath.

A moment goes by, and I'm still standing with my back against the door replaying the last few minutes of my life, thankful that they're over, until I slowly slide to the middle of the door and fix my right eye over the peep hole. He's still staring at my door. Startled, I quickly move my eye away from the little window. But after a second, I find myself gravitating toward the glass again. I watch as he picks up his newspaper and looks at my door one more time—and this time, I don't flinch. He looks my way for a second, arches one eyebrow and then turns and slides back inside his apartment.

God, Hannah was right. His eyes really are so blue, and his muscles are definitely...well, noticeable.

I close my eyes and for a second, I think about him and his blue eyes and his big muscles and his perfectly tanned skin. And I forget about my luck with neighbors and my big, awkward mouth and his staring obsession, until another image skips to the forefront of my mind and plops right down. It's of Suri at a table with her four cat-people sitting across from the Renaissance queen, a horse and a jousting stick. A sigh instantly follows.

"Damn it," I whisper to myself. "I wonder where he hides all his cats."

Chapter Seven

Keys

"He can't be dangerous," Hannah puffs. "They wouldn't let him live here, right? They check for that stuff—on the application?"

I think about it for a second.

"I guess. But maybe he's never been caught or he..."

"Lada," my sister scolds.

I hate her scolding voice.

"Not every guy has something wrong with him. So, he was weird when you first met him. Maybe he was just taken aback by your rugged, morning beauty."

I roll my eyes.

"Okay, well, if he's not a total weirdo, then I'm pretty sure I already scared him off anyway. Hannah, I might as well have been naked."

She forces out a laugh.

"Really, Lada?" Her voice has turned sarcastic. "You really think you scared him off by showing up at his door naked?"

I sigh loudly and try to push back a smirk. "You really would set me up with a convicted criminal, wouldn't you? You're that desperate, aren't you?"

"Hey, he hasn't been convicted...yet," she corrects.

Then, suddenly, there's a knock at the door, and we both freeze.

My lips part, and I feel my eyes grow wide as I immediately find Hannah. Her eyes are wide too, but she's smiling.

A second goes by like this—with neither of our expressions changing.

"See who it is," Hannah finally whispers, gesturing her finger toward the door.

I slowly turn and face the door, then tiptoe over to it and hover over the peep hole, and instantly, I feel my heart drop.

"It's him," I mouth, looking back at Hannah and pointing at the door.

"Who?" she asks.

"Next door," I whisper.

Just then, her face lights up, and she grabs her keys.

I shake my head.

"No," I mouth in her direction. "Do. Not. Leave. Me."

"I've gotta run," she says, ignoring me.

"Hannah," I say, trying my best to shout at her in a whisper.

She continues to ignore me, while I watch her run around my apartment and gather up her things. Leave it to Hannah to have a conversation with me about how my neighbor might be an axe murderer and then a minute later, she's leaving me alone with him. I sigh and roll my eyes.

"Okay, fine," I mumble under my breath.

I force my attention to the door and suck in some air. Then, on *three*, I push the air out of my lungs and swiftly pull open the door.

Jorgen takes a moment before he speaks.

"Your keys," he says, eventually, holding up his big hand and dangling a fuzzy, pink keychain from his finger. "You left them in your door."

My chest rises and then falls. Well, at least I'm making it easy for him to kill me.

"Hi, I'm Hannah, Lada's sister," Hannah says before I can even get the words *thank you* out.

She bumps up against me and extends her left hand toward him. Hannah's right-handed, and I would question what she's doing, but I already know.

"Lada?" he repeats, almost as if it's a question.

He pauses for a second but then seems to brush it off. "I'm Jorgen."

He meets her left hand with his left.

"Jorgen," Hannah says. "That's an interesting name."

He smiles. "It's a family name."

Hannah flashes him an approving look before she turns back to me.

"Invite him over," she mouths. "No ring."

I roll my eyes again, but this time, I only do it in my mind. And before I know it, Hannah is gliding down the stairwell.

"It was nice meeting you, Jorgen," she calls back up.

"It was nice meeting you too," he says in her direction before she's gone.

A moment passes and then Jorgen turns and looks at me with a soft side-smile.

"Lada?" he asks, almost timidly.

I lower my eyes and shake my head.

"It's a long story," I say.

"Okay," he concedes, chuckling a little.

"Paramedic?" I ask, eyeing his blue pants, white, collared shirt and black work boots.

He glances down at his attire.

"Uh, yeah." He nods his head. "How'd ya guess?"

A soft but unexpected laugh tumbles off my lips, sending my gaze straight to the floor.

"I work out of Truman Hospital."

His words sober me up fast, and I cringe on the inside.

"What do you do?" he asks.

I slowly meet his eyes again—those blue, blue eyes. "I write for the magazine downtown."

"*Outside*?"

"Yeah," I say.

"We get it at the hospital. Ada Cross?"

I feel the heat rushing to my face. It's not every day that someone puts my name to my writing.

"Yes," I say, trying not to smile as wide as I feel like smiling.

"I knew it was you." He pauses for a second, as if he's finally putting my face to my name. My photo has really only been in the magazine a couple times. Most of the time, it's just my byline on top of the story. "I like your people stories," he goes on. "There are some pretty interesting people out there."

I force out a laugh.

"You have no idea," I mumble.

His tanned, chiseled face shows off a crooked grin. "Well, I was just headed to work and I saw your keys," he says, pointing to my lock.

"Yeah." I shake my head. "Thank you," I add, squeezing the pink keychain inside the palm of my hand.

"No problem," he says.

I watch him start to make his way down the stairs.

"Lots of creeps out there, but don't worry, I've got your back," he calls up to me.

My smile starts to fade, but he can't see it; his back is already toward me.

I really hope that wasn't a warning—him warning me about himself. Deep down, I really don't want him to be a creep. Maybe I do just want a normal neighbor for once—a normal, cat-less, renaissance-less neighbor.

Chapter Eight

Remember

"**L**ada, where's your lotion?" Hannah asks, busting into my apartment.

Hannah's always been a fixture in every place I've ever had. She's never been an actual roommate, just more of an honorary one, I guess. This new apartment is no exception. She has a key. She uses it liberally.

"My hands feel like dead lizards." Her voice trails behind her as she makes a beeline for the back rooms.

I scrunch up my face. "Eww. Why do they have to be dead?"

She doesn't answer me. Instead I hear her rummaging through my drawers in my bedroom. My bedroom! I jump up and run to my room. But right when

I spot her, I freeze in the doorway. I know she has already seen it. She's bent over, with her back to me. She's staring at something—it—inside my nightstand drawer.

I just stand there and watch her—waiting, for what seems like an eternity.

Eventually, she pulls it out from the drawer and turns back toward me.

"Lada," she says, holding up a marriage license.

I take in a deep breath and let out an audible sigh.

"I didn't know you still had this," she softly says.

I don't say anything. There's nothing I can say really.

"Lada, you've got to move on," she pushes out, gently. "I know you love him, but he can't keep coming in and out of your life like this. You can't let him. You can't do this forever, Lada. You have to live."

She looks at me with two sad eyes—those same sad eyes that she always gives me when this same subject comes up.

"I am living, Hannah," I force out. "I'm living. I eat. I sleep. I smile every day."

Her sad eyes don't waver.

"Lada," she says and then follows it with a long sigh. "You know what I mean. You've gotta let him go. You've gotta let someone else in."

I stare at her for a moment before I lower my face. "It's not that easy, Hannah."

A minute passes in the quiet, and then I hear her voice again.

"All I'm asking you to do is try. That's all anyone is asking you to do."

My eyes catch and get stuck in the red polish on my toenails.

"I do try," I whisper.

It's true. I try. I don't try in the way she wants me to try, but I do try. I try to tell myself that it is possible to move on—that it is possible to actually live two happy lives in the span of one lifetime. I try to push the thoughts, the dreams, the nightmares from my old life to the back of my mind. But ultimately, I know what moving on means. It means never going back, and that terrifies me more than anything. I know Hannah wants me to forget, but I can't forget. I don't want to forget. If I forget, I lose it all twice. I want to remember. I have to remember.

Hannah's gone. She eventually got her lotion for her dead-lizard hands—after she had played the big-sister card, of course, and dispensed her infamous words of wisdom. I'm used to that card though and her words of wisdom. She says her peace—and it's usually always the same peace—and then she leaves it alone. I'm thankful for that—the leaving it alone part. She doesn't understand me like she thinks she does, but I do love her. Deep down, I know she means well. I just don't think I'm as strong as she thinks I am.

I rest my feet against the wooden railing on my little balcony and sit back in my Adirondack chair. The chair was a gift to me from my grandpa. He made it himself and gave it to me when I got my first place back in college.

I'm alone now. It's just me and the warm summer sun and a little, black spider crawling down a far rung in the railing. I'd freak out if I saw it inside, but I don't mind it so much out here. I watch it scurry across the painted wood, avoiding tiny roadblocks that I can't see. The spider reminds me of my grandpa's farm. There were always spiders there—spiders and mice and hay and tall grass and endless games of hide and seek. I think about those days when we were all just kids sometimes. And sometimes, I think about them so hard that I feel as if I'm there—in an open field with grass up to my waist and nothing but hours and hours before the summer sun goes down...

"James, you're on Hannah's team," Andrew says.

"But I was on Hannah's team last time," James protests. "You said I could be on Logan's team this time."

Hannah sends James her most serious look—the look of death.

"Like I want to be on your team, little squirt," Hannah says, piercing James with her narrowed eyes. "Andrew, why do you always get to pick the teams anyway?"

She turns her attention to Andrew.

"I'm the oldest," she continues. "I should pick, and I pick not to be on that little squirt's team. He's awful at this game."

"I'll be on his team," I say. "I'll be on James's team."

James is little. He can barely see over the grass. And he's slow, and he talks a lot. Hannah's right; he's not really very good at this game. But I feel bad for him.

"No," Andrew shouts. "I've picked the teams. It's already done. Hannah's with James. You're with me, Logan."

Everyone's quiet.

"Fine," Hannah puffs. "But this is the last time, Andrew, or I'm not playing anymore."

Andrew smiles proudly. James looks dejected but satisfied enough.

"Okay," Andrew says. "You guys count to sixty. Me and Logan are gonna go hide."

Andrew grabs my hand and takes off. I'm jolted forward, but I don't fall because Andrew has my hand and he's pulling me along. We run for a few seconds, but then suddenly, he stops and catches me as I almost fly face-first toward the ground.

"And no peeking," he yells back at Hannah and James. "And don't let James count."

"Nine, ten, eleven," Hannah shouts.

Andrew looks at me and smiles before we take off again. I wonder why he smiles. He must have a really good hiding place in mind.

We run and we run. We run across the field, cutting a jagged line through the tall grass. And every once in a while we backtrack and take a different way. I know Andrew does this to throw Hannah off. I feel pieces of the green stalks slide across my bare arms and legs as we flatten paths in the grass. It tickles my skin.

"Andrew, where are we going?" I ask, finally.

"The barn," he says.

My grandpa's farm is full of hiding places. We've hid in that old barn a million times.

"They'll find us there," I say.

"No, they won't."

I keep running, since I'm still attached to his hand, until we get to the barn and squeeze through a little space in a cracked, wooden door that reads Black Angus Farms *in old, faded letters across its front. I always imagine the letters being bright and pretty—the way they must have been a long, long time ago.*

It's musty inside the barn—dusty and full of big, sticky cobwebs. It looks like what I think an old dungeon would look like. I'd never be caught dead in here alone.

"Come on," Andrew says, pulling me along.

He runs to the other end of the barn and ducks his head when he gets to an old cattle chute.

"Watch your head," he calls back at me.

I duck my head under the wood and metal and let him pull me through.

We stop at the little, wooden slats that climb the wall to the hayloft.

"Up here." He reaches for a slat high above his head.

"Andrew, they'll find us up there. It's the first place they'll look."

"No, they won't," he says.

My shoulders slump, but after a second, I follow him up the ladder. And no sooner do I get a couple rungs off the barn floor, it starts raining dust and hay.

"Andrew, you're getting dirt in my hair!"

"What?" He angles his face down to look at me. "Oh. I can't help it. It's from the ladder."

I give him my best unhappy face. Then, I squeeze my eyes shut and lower my head as I climb the rest of the way through the dirt rain.

Andrew's already standing on the wooden floorboards of the hayloft when my head pops up through the hole in the floor.

"Jeez, Little Logan, you're a mess. What happened to you?" he asks, laughing.

I stop and narrow my eyes at him.

"You happened, Andrew."

He holds out his hand.

I crawl up another rung in the ladder. I think twice before giving him my hand, but I eventually do, and he yanks me toward him. The force of his pull sends me flying forward, and before I know it, I land with all fours onto the hard, wood boards.

"You okay?" he asks, bending down to me.

I look up at him. He looks weird all of a sudden—like he actually cares.

"Yeah," I say, standing up and brushing the dust and the hay out of my clothes and hair.

"Okay," he says. "Over here."

He grabs my hand and pulls me forward again. He pulls me to the corner of the barn and then slides behind a big, round hay bale.

"I'm not going back there," I protest.

"Come on. Don't be a scaredy-cat."

"No," I say, shaking my head and crossing my arms across my chest. "There are probably mice back there and spiders."

I really am scared. I really don't want to go back in that dark hole with all those creepy-crawly things.

Andrew puts out his hand, and his whole face changes.

"There are no mice," he says, gently. "And I'll protect you from the spiders."

I don't know why he's being so nice all of a sudden.

"Come on," he says, in the sweetest voice I've ever heard come out of Andrew Amsel.

I think about it for a couple more seconds. Then, I loosen one arm from around my chest and slowly hold my hand out to his.

His face lights up as he takes my hand.

I let Andrew lead me back behind the big bale, and together we crawl into a tiny corner and lower ourselves to the wood floor until our knees bend and press against our chests. It's dark except for a little ray of light that's pouring in through a hole in the wood on the side of the barn. And I'm still afraid of the mice and the spiders. I watch the dust dance in that little ray of light, hoping that Hannah and James hurry up and find us soon, until I feel Andrew squeeze my hand.

"Don't be scared," he whispers.

I take my gaze off the dust and the light and find Andrew's eyes. I can barely see them. They match the darkness around us.

He smiles, and it seems like a real smile this time. I look down because it kind of scares me too. What if he's been bitten by one of these spiders and he's going crazy or something?

"Logan," I hear him whisper.

I look up again, and this time, I notice his eyes on my lips.

"Wha...?" I start to ask.

Suddenly, his lips touch mine, stay there for a second and then pull away.

"We know you guys are in here," I hear Hannah yell.

I stiffen. She's in the hayloft now.

"What was that for?" I whisper to Andrew.

He just smiles at me.

I can hear Hannah's footsteps getting closer.

"Found you," Hannah yells.

Suddenly, Hannah is towering above us at the entrance to the little, dark space.

"I told her you guys would be in here," James shouts, coming up fast behind Hannah.

"Shut up, James," Hannah says. "I knew they'd be here too."

I look at Hannah and then at James and then I feel Andrew squeeze my hand. He shows off the little gap between his two front teeth and then steadies himself on one knee.

"All right," he says. "You found us. Your turn."

I watch Andrew crawl around me and then out of the little, dark hole. Then, he turns around and holds his hand out to me. I'm still confused, but I take his hand anyway and let him help me out of the mouse pit.

"Wait," James says. "You're not mad? We found you in like two seconds."

We all look at Andrew. Andrew just shrugs his shoulders, then sets his eyes on me.

"Nope," he says. "Couldn't be happier."

I slowly lift my gaze to Hannah and James, expecting their eyes to be on me. But they're not. They're both looking at Andrew like he needs a doctor. They're just standing there, motionless and silent, staring at him. And I'm just staring at them, wondering how much they had seen, until eventually, my gaze slowly falls back onto Andrew. He's smiling at me, and immediately, I think he might be crazy too. But then maybe I'm crazy because for the first time in my whole, entire life, I'm smiling back at Andrew Amsel— and there's no evil plot behind it.

Chapter Nine

The Quiet

"Hi."

I hear a smooth, deep voice come from behind me. I turn the key in the lock and swivel around.

"Oh, hi," I say.

I pull my bag's strap higher up my shoulder, and then a sound forces my attention to the stairs. It's the delivery guy, and I notice that he's also got Jorgen's attention now too. I watch as the boy-man in the George's pizza shirt and hat meticulously positions himself onto the metal stair railing and then slides all the way down it. I watch him until his feet hit the concrete and he scurries back to an older sedan with a little, lit-up

George's sign stuck to the roof before I turn my attention back to Jorgen.

He's already looking at me with a curious grin when I meet his eyes.

"He always does that," I say, waving it off.

Jorgen laughs and glances down at the pizza box in his hand.

"Dinner?" I ask.

"Yeah. Dishes are still packed."

I nod my head.

"You want some?" He extends the flat box a little toward me.

"Oh, no," I say. "Thanks though. I've got to meet someone for an interview in a few minutes."

I watch him nod his head now too. He really is intimidating somehow, and I think that's maybe why I feel so flustered around him. I'm not sure if it's his muscles and the fact that he could probably crush me with one hand if he really wanted to or if it's his piercing blue eyes and the way they seem to laser straight through me. Whatever it is, I've really got to get over it if I'm going to be living two yards away from him from now on.

"Another people story?" he asks, stopping my train of thought.

"Yep," I say.

I start my walk down the stairwell.

"A collector, strange addiction?"

I hear his voice trail behind me.

"I'm about to find out," I call back up to him.

I pull back into a parking space after the interview. It went an hour longer than I had anticipated, but I guess you've got a lot of years—and a lot of stories—between parachuting out of your first plane in World War II and downloading your first Johnny Cash song onto your iPod. I grab my bag off the passenger's seat and squeeze out of my door, being careful not to bang it against the car parked next to mine. These spaces are made for toys and Smart cars. I shimmy sideways and eventually make it out without a scratch—on me or the car—and head for the mailboxes in the breezeway.

"Hey," I hear a voice say as soon as I make it under the stairwell.

I look up.

"Jorgen. Hey, again."

He taps an envelope to his palm. "How'd the interview go?"

I think I seem unfazed on the outside, but on the inside, I'm secretly wondering if he somehow was able to stick a tracking device to me.

"It went well actually. Eighty-seven-year-old. Nice guy."

I look down to make sure I don't have any crumbs on my jeans from the granola bar I inhaled on the way back. When I look back up, Jorgen's staring at me with a questioning smile.

It takes me a second, but I eventually catch on.

"Steam-powered tractors," I say. "He has nine of them."

He nods his head. "To each their own."

I laugh in agreement and then find my tiny, metal box, stick my key into it and eventually pull out a newspaper from the next town over and a couple pieces of junk mail. But before I do that, I steal a glance at the name on the envelope in Jorgen's hand and memorize it. Then, I shove my mail into my bag and start my walk up the stairs. Jorgen follows me.

"How was dinner?" I ask, angling back toward him.

"Good." He's nodding his head. "A little quiet, but good."

I get to the top of the steps and stop in front of my door.

"Well, next time you get pizza, maybe you can bring it over," I say, shrugging one shoulder. "We could watch...the Food Network or something. Then it won't be so quiet."

I turn and push my key into the lock. What the hell did I just say? I swear there's something wrong with me. I open the door and slowly spin back around. He hasn't said anything, but he's got a boyish grin hanging off his lips and a questioning look plastered to his face.

"Really?" he asks, finally.

I think about it for a second. I could take it all back. I should take it all back. He's a stranger. And he might think I'm hitting on him. Am I hitting on him? No, I'm definitely not. *Make up an excuse!*

"Or I have some really girly movies," I offer.

He laughs. "I love the Food Network."

I could have taken it all back, but I didn't. There is definitely something seriously wrong with me.

"But you'll have to share," I add.

He's silent then—just long enough for me to realize that maybe I hate the quiet just as much as he does.

"That sounds nice," he says.

I'm not sure what "sounds nice" exactly—sharing, the lack of quiet over pizza or watching the Food Network. Any way, it doesn't matter. I'll probably regret this whole thing if it ever pans out later anyway.

"Well, have a good night," I say, stepping into my apartment.

"Good-night," I hear him say before I close the door behind me.

I quickly turn the lock on the dead bolt, then set my bag onto a barstool, bolt into the next room and plop down in front of my laptop. I'm on a mission.

I Google *Jorgen Ryker*—the name on the envelope—and then search the arrest records. After that, I search his name with his hometown and his name with the hospital he said he worked for. I search everything that might be connected to his name. And after an hour, all I've found is that he had a reserve champion steer at the state fair when he was thirteen and that his high school football team won the state championship his senior year. He was a running back, evidentially, and also not too shabby of an athlete, which is not that surprising judging by his arms and abs. But other than that, nothing—no arrests, no crazy or embarrassing photos on Facebook, no Twitter account. Nothing.

I rest my elbows onto the surface of my desk and stare into the screen and at an old, black and white newspaper photo of a gangly thirteen-year-old proudly standing next to a really, really big cow.

I take in a deep breath and then slowly force it out.

"Hmm. You're either really good at hiding your crazy, Jorgen Ryker, or maybe you really are just...normal."

Chapter Ten

Pizza

I hear a knock at the door, and I make my way over to the peep hole.

After one glance through the tiny window, my heart is racing. It's Jorgen, and he's holding a box of pizza.

I kind of figured he'd take me up on my offer. I just didn't expect it to be the next day. I run my fingers through my hair and look down at my outfit. I'm wearing sweatpants and a tee shirt. At least I have pants on this time. I push my lips to one side. There's pepper spray in a drawer in the kitchen, but as long as my professional stalking skills are up to par, I shouldn't be needing it. I count to three, and then I pull open the door.

"Hey," I say.

My eyes travel to the box in his hands.

"Didn't you just have pizza last night?" I ask, leaning up against the door.

He shrugs his shoulders. "The event tonight called for pizza."

I lower my eyes and push out a soft laugh.

"Well, you're just in time for a new episode of *Chopped*," I say, stepping back from the door.

He smiles wide. "Perfect."

I watch him step into my apartment and then hesitate a little before finally making his way to the couch.

"It looks nice in here," he says, his gaze sweeping the room. "You want to come over and decorate for me?"

I laugh again as I close the door and walk back into the kitchen. My heart is still racing. I'm praying to God he doesn't notice. *Just play it cool, Ada.*

"My sister did most of it. But I'm sure if you ask her, she'd be more than happy to do yours."

"Speaking of," he says. "What was it that she called you? Lada?"

I freeze with my hand on the knob of the cabinet door.

"Uh, yeah," I say.

I feel as if my words kind of clumsily stumble off my lips.

I pull two glasses out of the cabinet and catch him staring at the bookshelf and at a photo of Hannah and me.

"What's behind it?" he asks.

I swallow hard. The thought still stabs tiny holes into my heart.

"The name?" I ask.

"Yeah," he says, meeting my eyes.

I had hoped he wouldn't ask.

"Um, after eighteen, I started going by my middle name," I say and then pause.

He keeps his eyes on me.

"But my sister," I grudgingly continue, "being the creature of habit she is, had such a hard time dropping my first name that she just gave up and combined them."

He seems to think about something for a second.

"So, no one calls you by your first name anymore?"

"Uh, no," I say, shaking my head.

"So, what is it—your first name?" he asks.

My heart almost jumps right out of my chest. I'm not sure why. I've said my name a million times before, when I had to—when the law required.

"It's Logan," I say. My voice is barely audible.

"Logan," he repeats. "That's a pretty name."

He continues to look at me as if he wants me to explain why I don't use it.

Instead, I grab two plates, scoop up the glasses and head toward him.

"So, do you have any brothers or sisters?" I ask.

There's a slight hesitation before he speaks.

"One sister. She lives in Connecticut with her husband. I don't really see her as much as I'd like."

"Well, what took her to Connecticut?"

"Her husband's job," he says. "He's an engineer."

"Oh," I say, as I take a seat on the other side of the couch.

"You?" he asks.

I look at him with a rascally side-smile.

"My husband's not an engineer," I say.

He takes a second to study my face, then laughs.

"No, any brothers or sisters besides Hannah?" he asks.

"No," I confirm. "Just me and Hannah."

I hand him a plate, and he picks up a piece of pizza and sets it onto my plate.

I feel like he shouldn't be that comfortable with me—comfortable enough to touch my food—but strangely, I don't mind all that much.

"Thanks," I say.

I feel my face turning bashful all of a sudden.

"The guy with the beard's going to win."

My eyes follow a line to the TV and then back to him. "How do you know?"

"I just know," he says. "It's all in the way they chop their vegetables. The best vegetable chopper wins—always."

I laugh. "That's not true."

"Just watch," he says. "You'll see."

I surrender and silently agree to play along.

"So what made you move to Columbia?" I ask after a moment.

"The job," he says. "It was an offer I couldn't pass up, I guess you'd say."

I nod my head.

"So, how long have you been a paramedic then?"

He finds my eyes.

"If I didn't know better, I'd say you were some kind of reporter for some big magazine or something."

I lower my eyes and feel a shy smile tugging at the corner of my mouth.

"Sorry," I say. "I can't help it."

He laughs. "It's fine. I'll answer anything you ask."

My gaze eventually finds his again.

"I've been a paramedic for about four years now," he says. "I started here in Columbia."

I pause for a second to quickly add up the years. I guess he's a couple years older than me—maybe twenty-four or twenty-five.

"Did you always want to be one?"

"A paramedic?" he asks.

"Yeah," I confirm.

He lowers his head and chuckles.

"No. I wanted to be a chef. But I learned early on that I wasn't very good at it. Plus, it's not really a real career where I come from."

Now, it's my turn to study his face.

"You don't sound too broken up about not starring on this show," I say, at last, pointing at the TV.

He laughs again. "I'm not. I love what I do. I meet a lot of interesting people. Kind of like yourself, I guess."

This time, a smile instinctively finds my face.

"Yeah, kind of like me," I agree.

"What about you?" he asks. "When did you know you wanted to be a famous writer?"

I glance up at him, and I know I have that bashful look on my face again. It's a side effect of being around him, I'm starting to believe. I try to play it off nonetheless.

"Famous?" I say. "Not sure I know what that's like yet. But a writer—that would have been at twenty, I think. I decided somewhere in my second year of college. It just kind of came to me while I was staring at a Shakespeare quote one day. I had never really written much of anything before that."

He cocks his head in my direction.

"So, I'd never dig up any childhood memoirs or deep philosophical poems you wrote when you were seven?" he asks.

I laugh and shake my head.

"Not a one," I confirm.

A silent moment passes as our laughter fades.

"I never really thought about careers when I was younger," I say.

I notice his eyes stumble onto mine again.

"Well, what did you think about?"

"I don't know." I hesitate a little. "Being happy, I guess."

I stop at that. I don't say happy with whom. I don't mention the house in the country. I don't mention the three kids we would never have together or the fifty years we would never see.

"Sounds like a pretty good thing to think about," he says.

A broken smile finds my lips.

"See," he suddenly says.

His eyes are planted on the TV now. There's one guy left standing on the show. It's the guy with the beard.

I flash him a suspicious grin. "How did you know that?"

"It's all in the chop," he says, casually. "You want another piece?"

I think about it, then lower my eyes. "Sure."

He slides another piece of pizza onto my plate.

"So, do you make it home much?" I ask.

"Uh, yeah." I watch him grab another slice for himself. "About once a month or so. My buddy plays on a softball league, and I play the fill-in sometimes when I can."

I nod my head as my eyes travel back to the television.

"The girl with the tattoos."

"What?" I ask.

"She wins," he says.

He takes another bite of pizza and then arches one eyebrow at me. "Watch her chop."

And I do just that. I watch the girl covered in tattoos meticulously for a minute. She's fast, and she seems efficient, but I still don't believe him. And soon, I find my attention wandering away from the television and back onto the man beside me. He seems too good to be true. And blame it on my odd curiosity, my past experiences or my job, for that matter, but I just can't stop wondering what his weird thing is. It probably would have been better to find that out before I invited him to sit next to me on my couch in my apartment, but I guess it's better late than never.

"What's your strangest habit?" I blurt out.

He stops and fixes his eyes on me—long enough for me to start to feel a little uncomfortable.

"I see dead people," he whispers low and mysteriously.

His expression is as straight as it can be. Mine, on the other hand, goes completely blank, and it stays like that until I see his lips start to crack across his face.

"Jorgen," I exclaim. "You can't joke about things like that with me. I've met people who really do believe they see dead people."

He starts to laugh.

"Really?" he manages to get out.

"Yes, and people who believe that people come back as cats and..."

"As cats?" he interjects.

The way he sounds so honestly surprised makes me laugh too. "Yes, cats."

"Like in an afterlife?" he asks.

I nod my head in confirmation.

"Who believes that?"

He asks it as if he still doesn't believe me.

"I had a neighbor in college. All four of her cats were on their second lives."

He stops laughing, and it almost looks as if he's going to be successful at regaining at least some composure, until he cracks, and the laughter just starts pouring from his lips again. His laugh is raspy, deep, kind of sexy and also kind of contagious.

"One was even a TV meteorologist," I say, holding up a finger.

He rubs tears from his eyes. I, on the other hand, manage to gain control of myself and take another bite of pizza.

"It's true," I say.

He eventually calms down and takes a drink. Then, he slowly sets the glass back down onto the coffee table.

"M&M's," he says.

I look up. "What?"

"Every Sunday, I go to the same gas station down the street and buy a pack of M&M's, and I eat all of them except for the green ones."

I feel my eyebrows instinctively furrowing.

"Why?" I ask.

"It goes back to when I was a kid," he says. "When my sister and I were little and my parents would stop at the gas station, they'd always let us get a bag of candy to share. And we'd always get M&M's. Then, once we got in the car, we'd divvy them up. She got the green ones. I got the rest."

"That doesn't sound very fair."

"That's all she wanted," he says, shrugging his shoulders. "They were the best, evidently."

"Okay," I say. "So what do you do with the green ones now? Do you just...throw them away?"

He stops and shakes his head.

"No, I mail them to my sister the next day."

I start to laugh but then notice his face is completely sober.

"Wait." I cover my mouth. "You're serious?"

"As a heart attack," he says.

"So, your sister gets a bag of green M&M's every week?"

"Yeah," he says, chuckling. "Pretty much."

"That's kind of cute," I say. "Strange, but cute."

He shrugs his shoulders.

"Your turn."

I feel my chest rise as I take a breath and think about it for a second.

"I don't know," I say.

His eyes find mine, and one side of his mouth turns into a crooked grin. It's kind of endearing. "You do everything backwards."

I feel my eyes narrowing and my eyebrows slowly making their way toward each other again, but I don't say anything.

"You eat your pizza crust-first," he continues, eyeing my half-eaten piece of pizza.

I look down at my plate. Sure enough, there's a little triangle left—with no crust.

"You read your newspaper backwards," he goes on.

I cock my head to the side.

"When I first met you, you turned to the back page first. Even your name is backwards," he points out.

I bite the side of my bottom lip. "Those aren't so strange, are they?" I ask, timidly.

He laughs.

"Nah. Now, when you start walking backwards, I'm taking you straight to live with that cat lady."

I laugh, and at the same time, try to keep myself from blushing as I force my eyes back to the television screen. We both watch the show on it for a little while longer then until his voice breaks my concentration.

"Look," he says, pointing at the TV. "What did I tell you?"

On the screen, there's one woman left standing in front of the judges, and her arms are covered in tattoos.

My smile starts small and eventually stretches across my face. I'm starting to believe he might be on to something.

"Thanks for letting me come over."

He's standing on the other side of my door now, three steps from his own.

"Pizza's a lot better when it's not so quiet," he adds.

I push out a laugh. "I agree."

And just then, he brings his face so close to mine that his lips are nearly touching my ear. My heart starts racing, and for the first time around him, my stomach seems to do a somersault. It feels like butterflies, and it's terrifying and a little sad, I think. But I can smell the soft, sweet scent of his cologne, and it seems to calm me somehow. I know I should be weirded out right now—I have no idea what he's doing—but this feels good, and I can't stop smiling this nervous, happy, strange smile.

"They were reruns," he whispers, his breaths trailing over my skin.

I freeze as my mouth falls open and surprise quickly devours my face. "I didn't believe you for one second," I say, shaking my head.

He shoots me a suspicious look. "Not one second?" he asks, backing slowly away from me.

I try my hardest to scold him with my eyes, even though every other feature is betraying me.

"Good-night, Miss Cross," he says, sliding a key into his lock and pushing open his door.

I lower my eyes and softly laugh to myself. "Good-night," I say.

Chapter Eleven

The Photo

"Coming," I call out from across my apartment.

I don't even bother looking at the peep hole this time. I figure its either Hannah or possibly Jorgen. For all I know I left my keys in the door again. But when I pull open the door and look up, I freeze.

"Amsel," I manage to get out.

I don't know when I started calling him by his last name to his face. Somewhere along the line, it just kind of happened. I step back to let him inside.

"I can't stay long," he immediately says, taking a step forward. "I really have to run. I just, um, found something I thought you might want."

He holds out a photograph.

"You know I love you, Logan—Ada," he quickly corrects.

My heart stings in my chest. There are two hands in the photo, each wearing a ring.

"I know," I say, taking the photo and lowering my eyes to it.

We stand there for a while. I don't even know how much time passes. We're both so still. My eyes are on the photo. His eyes are most likely on me, watching for my reaction. I try not to react—for his sake and mine.

After a moment, he breaks the silence.

"Well, I've got to go."

He reaches out and touches my hand.

"Take care, Ada."

I look into his eyes. I love those eyes. I miss those eyes.

"You sure you don't want something to drink or anything?" I ask, as he takes a step back toward the door.

"No, I'm sorry, I really am running late. I just found that yesterday and wanted you to have it."

I look down at the photo again and sigh. This is the first time I've ever seen it.

"Okay," I say, nodding my head. "Thank you," I add.

I follow him to the door, and when he opens it, Jorgen is just opening his door across the hall.

I watch as Jorgen eyes Amsel up and down once, then steps outside and closes his door behind him. He waits there, facing us. He looks as if he's not trying to make it obvious that he's watching the two of us, but somehow, I know he is. Amsel too takes a good look at Jorgen. Then, he turns and glances at me.

I try to conjure up a faint smile to let him know it's okay.

He glances back at Jorgen. There's a look on Amsel's face. I can't tell if it's simply a greeting or more like a warning. Either way, Amsel nods his head once and makes his way to the stairs.

I follow Amsel's figure down the stairwell until he's out of sight. And when I look back up at Jorgen, I realize he was doing the same thing—following Amsel. His eyes are still planted on the stairs. I take the opportunity to steal another glance at the photo, and then I quickly slide it into the pocket of my hooded sweatshirt.

"Who was that?" Jorgen asks, curiously.

It takes me a second to answer him. I have to retrieve my mind from a different time first.

"A friend," I say, as I toss my gaze to the ground.

I look back up a second later, and Jorgen's eyes are still on me. He looks at me like he wants to believe me. I think I look at him like I want him to believe me too.

It wasn't completely a lie. Amsel is my friend, but he's also a whole lot more than that.

Jorgen seems as though he wants to say something, but he doesn't, until I turn to go back inside my apartment.

"Hey," he says, stopping me. "I have this work barbeque tomorrow night. You maybe wanna come with me?"

I rotate around and catch his pleading blue eyes—the same pleading blue eyes that have no idea that at twenty-two, I've already lived one life and am now on my second. I feel my heart beating a hard, fast rhythm against my chest, but I think it's his pleading, clueless blue eyes that make me nod my head *yes* in spite of my heart.

"Sure," I say.

He slowly bobs his head up and down a couple times.

"Good," he says, through what seems like a happy grin. "I'll pick you up at six."

I force my lips up and then push through my door and close it behind me. And before I know it, my back, minus any thought, is pressing against the back of the door. I feel my body slide down until I'm kneeling on my heels. And just like that, a familiar, warm liquid pushes past my eyelids and streams down my cheeks. I can't stop it. I have no reason to stop it—alone and inside my apartment, tucked away from the world. I feel my heart growing heavy as I pull out the photo from my sweatshirt's pocket and let my eyes search every detail—the little diamond, the two wedding bands, the scar on his middle finger from a run-in with a barbed wire fence when he was eleven. And I let my mind drift away until I feel breakable—like I could shatter into a million, tiny pieces right where I'm kneeling.

We spend so much of our passion on our first love. I'm not convinced that it—passion—is one of those things that you have an endless amount of—like happiness or sadness. I could be happy all day. I could be sad all day. But I'm not so sure I'll ever love like that again.

I quickly wipe a tear off the photo with my sleeve and then let my head fall into my bended knees.

I think I used all my passion up on the boy who stole my first *I love you*...

A thunderous bang crashes in the heavens and then rumbles over the earth. We all look up at the sky. Huge, dark clouds are gathering right above us.

"Tut-tut, it looks like rain," Hannah shouts from the outfield.

Andrew turns the baseball over in his hand and then rests it in his glove.

"Come on. We've got at least ten more minutes," he shouts. "James, you're up to bat."

James looks terrified as he stares up at the dark sky and twists the barrel of his wooden bat into the dirt.

"Come on, James. Don't be a little squirt. Get in the box," Hannah shouts.

James's chest rises and then falls before he slowly shuffles to the batter's box and positions himself in front of me.

"It's all right, James," I say to him from behind my catcher's mask. "Just hit the ball, and then we'll all go inside."

James nods his head and then slowly faces Andrew on the pitcher's mound. Andrew winds up and releases the ball. It comes fast and whizzes right through the strike zone.

James swings, but the ball misses his bat and lands in my mitt instead. I stand up and throw the ball back to Andrew, and at the same time, feel a drop on my hand. I glance up at the sky and then down at James.

"Okay, James, you'll get this next one," I say.

I kneel down again and wait for the second pitch.

"I felt a drop," Hannah yells from the outfield. "I'm outta here. I'm not letting this mess up my beachy waves."

And just like that, we're all watching Hannah sprint across the field and toward the house like a crazy person.

I catch Andrew through the bars in my mask a second later. He's already facing the batter's box again, paying no attention to his outfielder who just left him. I watch his windup and then, for the second time, he releases the ball. And once again, James swings, but the ball flies unscathed right into my mitt.

"It's all right, James," I say. "That's why we get three tries. Just try to keep your eye on the ball."

I stand up and throw the ball back to Andrew. Then, all of a sudden, another crash of thunder rumbles through the sky, but this time, it seems to shake the earth around us.

James flashes me a frightened glance, then looks up at the sky. "I'm outta here too!" he yells, throwing the bat to the ground.

He takes off running toward the house. I slide the catcher's mask off and look up. There's nothing but big, dark, ominous clouds above us now.

"Play catch with me," Andrew says, trying to win me over with his puppy-dog-pleading eyes.

I just stare at him. I know it's about to pour.

"Come on," he begs.

I let out a sigh, but somehow, there's a smile attached as I set the mask and the catcher's mitt onto the ground, slide a glove over my hand and open it toward him.

"Yes," he exclaims, pumping his fist.

He throws the ball, and it lands hard inside my glove. But before I can even get the ball into my opposite hand, the sky opens up, and a flood of water traps us in its wake.

I can't help but squeal. The big drops washing over my skin are ice-cold.

Andrew runs over to me and scoops up the mask, the mitt and the bat and throws them into a five-gallon bucket. Then, he slides the glove off my hand and throws it into the bucket as well right before he grabs my hand.

"Come on," he says, pulling me along.

We run to a little shed next to the dirt field and take shelter under it. Inside, I wipe my eyes and unglue the hair stuck to the sides of my face, then cross my arms around my chest to ward off the goose bumps.

Andrew sets the bucket in the corner, then comes over to me and puts his arms around my shoulders and starts rubbing the parts of my bare skin that aren't covered by my tee shirt.

I feel a shiver run up my back right before I look up at him. "Thanks," I say.

For a second, it's as if his eyes are stuck in mine. Then, slowly, a smile zigzags across his face.

"Jeez, Little Logan, you look like a wet, little kitten. What happened to you?"

I roll my eyes and wrap my arms tighter around my chest. "You happened, Andrew."

He laughs.

"You know what?"

"What?" I ask.

I grab the bottom of my tee shirt and twist it until water starts to come out.

"I love you."

I immediately drop my shirt and jerk my head up.

"What did you say?"

"I...I love you."

I bore two holes straight through his head, but his expression doesn't waver. "No, you don't." I look away and laugh nervously. Then, I decide quickly that battling the rain just might be less awkward than the conversation we're apparently having right now, and I take a step out into it.

"Wait," Andrew says, grabbing my arm and pulling me back. "Where are you going?"

"Home," I say.

He's somehow successful at getting me back inside the shed.

"Just wait a second. What do you mean I 'don't'?"

"I mean, you don't know what love is. You're twelve, Andrew."

"Twelve and half," he corrects me.

"Fine," I say. "It still doesn't matter. I'm twelve and a half too, and I don't even know what it means."

I pull my hand back and start out of the shed again.

"Wait," he says, grabbing my arm and pulling me back yet again.

He looks at me with that little devilish grin he gets sometimes, and for the first time, I notice that the little gap that used to be between his two front teeth is gone.

"What makes you think that just because we're twelve, we don't know what love is?"

I try to show him how annoyed I am by forcing my free arm to my hip. "We're just kids."

Andrew laughs once.

"Speak for yourself. I'm a man."

Without even thinking, I bust out laughing.

Andrew just stands there—straight-faced. "Well, at least I got you to laugh."

I smile and shake my head back and forth.

"I love you, Logan," he says again.

He releases my arm, and immediately, I cross it with my other arm over my chest.

"And you wanna know how I know I love you?" he asks.

I stare at him for a second and then playfully roll my eyes. Butterflies have somehow gotten into my stomach, but there's no way I'm letting him know that.

"I'll take that as a yes," *he says, flashing me a wink.*

I really try hard not to blush.

"I know because when I see you, I smile. I know because when I'm not with you, you're all I can think about. I know because when I hear good news, you're the first person I want to tell. And I know because when I hear bad news, you're the first person I want to talk to."

He's quiet for a few moments then. I am too. I feel stunned—as if for the first time in my life, I just have no words. And I just can't seem to take my eyes off the packed dirt that makes up the shed floor at my feet either. I'm too nervous to look up at him. Just a year ago, I think I would have rather died than admit this, but I kind of liked what he said, and I'm scared he might take it all back.

"You're right, though," he says.

His words grab my attention, and I slowly turn my eyes up to his again. Please don't take it all back.

"I've never been in love before, but if this isn't love, what else could it be?" he asks.

I'm quiet until I realize that all the things he said he feels, I feel too. It's not really a revelation. I think I knew it all along. I just never dared say it out loud.

"Andrew." I can barely hear myself talk—maybe it's the rain or maybe it's because I can't believe what I'm about to say.

He meets my gaze.

"I think I'm in love too," I whisper.

I hold my breath for a whole long, agonizing second before a cheesy grin stretches wide across his face.

"Come on," he says, pulling me out into the rain.

"What? No, Andrew, what are you doing?"

The rain looked pretty good a minute ago—when I just wanted to get away. Now, not so much.

We get a few steps away from the shed before he stops, and the downpour instantly engulfs us. I can barely see him through the big, icy drops sliding down my face and hanging on my eyelashes. But I feel him squeeze my hand, and then he turns toward the field and I notice his chest rise as he inhales a big breath of air and then shouts at the top of his lungs: "I love Logan Cross."

He looks at me when he's finished. That big, silly grin hasn't left his face. His hair is pressed down and dripping. There are raindrops on his eyelashes. His clothes are drenched and hanging off of him. It makes me laugh, and all of a sudden, I'm tasting the salty raindrops in my mouth. I swallow and laugh some more, then take a deep breath and shout as loud as I can: "I love Andrew Amsel."

And just like that, I don't feel the chill in the raindrops anymore. I don't feel the weight of my rain-soaked clothes, and I'm no longer blinded by the big, salty drops clouding my vision. Because somehow, I can still see Andrew's big brown eyes smiling back at me, and right now, that's all that seems to matter.

Chapter Twelve

Barbeque

It's 5:45. I literally just walked in the door.

I throw my bag onto the couch and run to the closet in my room. There's a bright sundress staring back at me. I grab it and change out of the slacks and button-up top I wore to work and into the dress. I spot a pair of flip flops in the corner of the room. I hurry over to the shoes and force my feet into them before I run to the bathroom, throw on a pair of stud earrings and touch up my make-up. My hair is up. I take it down and spray some hair spray on it. But I think most of the spray goes into the air and then into my nose and mouth instead. I'm coughing and fanning the air with my hand when I hear a knock at the door. And instantly, I feel my heart skip a beat. I look into the mirror and then at the mess I've made with my make-up on the counter. I ignore it—there's no time—and I quickly grab some lip gloss and shove it into a clutch. And within seconds, I'm making my way to the door. But just before I open it, I stop and run my fingers through my hair one more time. I'm nervous. I've told myself all day that this is not a date. I wasn't exactly thinking clearly when I agreed to it. This can't be a date. I can't date. And he's just a friend—practically a stranger.

I pull open the door, and Jorgen immediately eyes me up and down once.

"You look...good." He has a wide grin on his face. I can't tell if he's being sincere or sarcastic.

I let out a frazzled sigh. "I just got home fifteen minutes ago."

"Well, you look great," he says.

I can tell it's definitely sincere this time, even though "great" isn't exactly what I'd call myself right now.

"You look nice too," I say, well aware that I'm starting to blush.

He's wearing khaki cargo shorts and a gray, fitted tee shirt—one in which I can't help but notice his muscles.

"Well, you ready?" he asks.

I try to hide my bashful state. I still haven't figured out why his muscles make me feel so unraveled.

"Yeah," I say.

I reach back and grab the keys off the counter and pull the door closed behind me before following him down the stairs and to the parking lot.

"I hope you don't mind," he says. "My truck's in the shop. I've only got my bike right now."

I look up from shoving my keys into my clutch and stop cold.

"I have an extra helmet," he says. "It was my sister's."

I don't say anything. I just stare at the bike and then at him holding the helmet.

"Ada?" I think I hear him say after a moment.

"Um," I stutter. "You know what? We can just take my car." I reach inside my clutch and recover my keys. "It's not a problem," I quickly rattle off.

He's quiet, and a few long seconds pass us by before I eventually look up and find his eyes. They look sad or confused or something.

"It's safe," he tries to assure me. "I promise. The barbeque is just right down the road. I'll go slow. It'll be fun."

My eyes fall heavy to the ground at my feet.

"I'm wearing a dress," I say, sheepishly.

"Oh," he says and then stops. "Right. I'm sorry. I should have said something earlier."

"It's fine," I manage to get out. "I'll just drive. It's not a big deal. I'm parked over here."

I command my legs to move, and I start out toward my car.

"I'm really sorry, Ada," he says, as he catches up to me. "I didn't mean for you to drive. I just thought it would be fun to ride the bike."

"It's really fine," I say, forcing a laugh. "It's really not the end of my world if I drive. There's no reason for you to be sorry."

I stop at the car, and he does too, and quickly, his eyes lock onto mine. And all of a sudden, I can't seem to look away or move or do anything, as I watch a soft, crooked smile edge up his face.

"I can't help it, Ada. You really shouldn't have shown up at my door without pants on the first time I met you."

I know I can't hide the red rushing to my face, but I do try my hardest to fight the nervous smile that is attached to it. God, what have I gotten myself into? This is definitely a date.

"You can put the helmets in the back," I say, flashing him the smile that ultimately won the battle.

He chuckles and sets the helmets onto the seat.

"So, where are we going?" I ask as I pull open the door.

"Broadway Park," he says.

I get in and wait for him to slide into the passenger's seat next to me. After he does, I shift the gear into reverse and catch a glimpse of the helmets in the rearview mirror. One's black; the other's pink. I suck in a deep breath and then slowly exhale. *God, really, what have I gotten myself into?*

"Kev, this is Ada," Jorgen says, introducing me to a man who's maybe in his late twenties. "Ada, Kevin.

I meet Kevin's outstretched hand with my own.

"Nice to meet you," I say.

"The pleasure's all mine." He has somewhat of a country twang to his voice—not Southern, just country.

Kevin is one of those guys who kind of reminds me of a teddy bear. He's not super round or anything. I mean, he's not nearly as chiseled as Jorgen, but he's not really overweight either. He's just a little shorter and a little heavier than average—a teddy bear, a sandy blond teddy bear. And he's squinting his eyes at me.

"You know, you look kinda familiar for some reason," he says, searching my face.

I turn my attention to Jorgen. "I feel like I've gotten that a lot lately."

Jorgen is staring at Kevin and has a look on his face as if he's in deep thought or something.

"She's Ada Cross," Jorgen says after a second. "She writes the people stories in *Outside*."

Kevin looks at me again and then starts slowly nodding his head. "You know, that's probably it."

For some reason, he doesn't look completely convinced.

"Well, wow. I've never met anyone famous before," he goes on, refitting the baseball cap on his head.

A laugh unexpectedly escapes me.

"Famous?" I say. "You guys really need a new standard for *famous*."

"Well, I've never had my name in anything," Kevin says. "Good or bad."

Just then, Jorgen puts his arm around Kevin. "Now, Ada, you could actually write a pretty good story about this guy."

Kevin stands in his place, smiling proudly all of a sudden.

"This guy just might be the strangest person I've ever met."

The sandy blond teddy bear seems unfazed by Jorgen's mention of the word *strange*.

"Am I right, Kevin?"

Kevin shrugs his shoulders and then nods his head.

"This guy has some kind of weird photographic memory," Jorgen continues. "I mean he can remember the smallest of details and the most common of faces."

I take a second and squint one eye playfully.

"Really?" I ask.

"I can't remember everything," Kevin modestly confesses. "But I can remember faces pretty good. If I've seen a face even for a few seconds, then nine out of ten times, I remember it."

I cock my head a little to the side. "Then where have you seen mine?"

He seems to be a little taken aback as I hold my stare in his.

"It's...uh...not completely foolproof. You might be the exception." He looks nervous all of a sudden.

I start to laugh. "I'm just joking with you. I wish I could remember faces better. That sounds like a pretty cool strange trait to have."

I watch the life slowly return to Kevin's face.

"Hey, Kevin, these your brats over here?"

We all turn our attentions to a voice coming from a pavilion in the center of the park.

Kevin grabs the bill of his cap and adjusts the hat over his head again. "Well, it looks like I've got some brats that need tendin' to. It was nice meeting you, Ada."

"It was nice to meet you too," I say.

Kevin playfully punches Jorgen in the arm and then trots off toward the pavilion. We watch him until he reaches a barbeque grill and plants his feet behind it.

"He's a pretty good guy," Jorgen says, regaining my attention. "I've worked right alongside him ever since I got the job here."

I slowly nod my head. "He seems nice."

My eyes trail off to Kevin under the pavilion again for a moment, until I feel Jorgen's eyes on me.

"What?" I ask, starting to laugh.

"Nothing," he says. "I'm just glad you're here."

I don't say anything. I just flash him a playful smile.

"You want any more to eat?"

I shake my head. "I think I'm good."

"You wanna walk?" he asks, gesturing toward the trail behind us.

My eyes wander to the trail and then back to him. "Sure."

We start off toward the base of the little, white-graveled path, which wraps around the park. I've run on the same trail a few times before, but I've never walked it with anyone.

"So, did you go to college here?"

I glance up at him and nod my head. "I did. Mizzou."

"Aah," he says. "They're known for that—what you do," he states and sort of asks at the same time.

I slowly nod my head some more. "Yeah, they are," I confirm. "What about you?" I ask.

"Oh, I got my paramedic license at a small school back home." He steals a quick glance at me. "It's not world-renowned or anything."

I think I get stuck in his crazy blue eyes for a second. I would call them ice-blue, but they're not at all cold.

"Well, I'm sure you're great at what you do even so," I say. "You work for a pretty respected hospital."

Jorgen's expression instantly turns bashful, and his gaze falls to the ground as we walk a few more steps in silence.

"I was wearing pants," I say, eventually.

He stops walking and sends me a questioning look.

"That first time we met, I was wearing boxers—shorts," I quickly correct myself.

He starts to grin, and then he sets out down the trail again. "I'm still going to remember it as no pants."

I lower my head and laugh softly to myself.

"In my head," he continues, "the first time I met you, your hair was down; you were wearing a big sweatshirt and nothing else; and you promised me that you weren't a former one-night stand."

"Oh my gosh," I exclaim. "Please don't."

"Can't undo a memory," he says, laughing. "Plus, it was perfect. You don't know how many times I had dreamed about something like that happening to me."

I playfully shove him. His shoulder is strong and hard, and it's the first time since shaking his hand that I've touched him, I quickly realize.

He pretends to be affected by my harmless strike as he shrinks to one side.

"I had hoped that you were weird—like four-cats-with-past-lives weird," I confess.

"What?" he asks. "Why?"

"I don't know." I shake my head. "That's what I was used to, I guess—people living in their own little worlds while I lived in mine. It makes life pretty easy that way. People like that don't care if you show up at the door wearing a clown suit or naked, much less pantless."

His powder blues meet mine.

"What?" I ask, playfully narrowing my eyes.

"I never said I cared either," he says.

I match him—stare for stare—until a wild grin shoots across his face.

"No, I'm kidding," he says. "Sort of," he adds. "No." He shakes his head. "I'm not kidding at all. I don't care what you show up at my door wearing, as long as you show up."

I start to laugh, and he does too. We laugh together for several moments, until our laughter fades and Jorgen turns to me.

"You know, there's something about you, Ada Cross." He looks at me through hooded eyes. "What are you doing for dinner Monday night?"

I'm quiet for a second, but on the inside, I'm panicking.

"I'm working late," I say.

His smile starts to fade.

"What about Wednesday?" I offer.

I've seriously gone off the deep end. I don't even know what my mouth is saying anymore.

His broad chest rises and then falls.

"I work until eight, and I wouldn't have time to make anything."

"Perfect," I say. "I'll make us dinner. You brought dinner last time."

He looks happy again. "I brought a box of pizza."

I toss him a sarcastic grin. "I'm not promising much more than that."

Soft laughter falls from his lips. I like his laugh. There's something strangely sexy about it.

"That still sounds really nice," he says.

I think I feel my face light up because it does sound nice. It shouldn't sound nice, but it does. And if this isn't a date, I'm pretty sure Wednesday night will be. I really don't know what I'm getting myself into. I might as well be walking through my life backwards. At least then I'd have an excuse.

We're suddenly at the end of the trail. It's almost dark now, and there are only a few cars left in the parking lot.

"Hey, Jorgen, there you are."

We both hear Kevin yell from across the park, so we stop and wait for him to catch up to us. It takes him a couple seconds, but he eventually does and swings his arm around Jorgen's shoulder.

"Hey, you bring your truck?" Kevin asks. "I think I left my sunglasses in there the other day."

Jorgen shakes his head. "Ada drove. Truck's in the shop."

"Well, why didn't you take her for a ride on your bike? It's a good night for it." Kevin's gaze eventually lands on me, and immediately, his whole demeanor changes.

I catch the strange look in his eyes and try to stop my face from instinctively crumpling into some kind of confused mess.

"The dress," Jorgen says, simply.

Kevin's attention quickly leaves me and travels straight to the ground at his feet. It takes him a minute, but then he nods his head. "Right," he says, allowing his eyes to venture my way again. "I'm sorry."

I shrug my shoulders and force a smile. Kevin finally smiles, but it seems forced too.

"Well, can you bring them to work?" Kevin asks, returning his attention to Jorgen. "The sunglasses."

"Sure," Jorgen says.

"Well, all right, you two have fun tonight." Kevin pats Jorgen on the shoulder. "And Ada...again, it was...uh...nice to meet you."

I wave at Kevin, but I keep a suspicious eye on him as he walks away.

"I'll see ya," Jorgen says to him before turning back to me. "You ready?"

My stare quickly breaks from Kevin. "Uh, yeah."

I unlock the car, and Jorgen opens my door for me. Instantly, my eyes go to his, and I flash him that silly, bashful smile again. I'm learning I really can't help it.

"Thanks," I say and slide into the driver's seat.

He gently closes the door and then makes his way over to the passenger's side, while I steal another quick glance back at Kevin. He's talking to someone else now across the parking lot. His back is to me, so he can't see me. I keep my stare on him for several moments before Jorgen at last falls into the seat next to mine.

"Where's Kevin from?" I ask, sticking the key into the ignition.

"Uh, Moberly," Jorgen replies.

"Hmm." I mumble the word out loud but mostly to myself. "Does he really remember every face?"

I turn and catch Jorgen's blue, blue eyes.

"I know it's weird, but for the most part, he does," he says.

I feel my eyebrows starting to collide into each other again as another thought grazes the tip of my mind, but Jorgen's lips edging up his handsome face stops the thought cold.

"Thanks for coming with me tonight, Ada."

I feel my features soften.

"It was fun," I say and mean it.

"Well, this is me." I stop at my door.

Jorgen is holding the two helmets—one in each hand. We're both staring at each other when I finish my sentence. I don't know what to do next.

"Good-night, Ada," he says, before I can think of something else to do.

I let go of a thankful breath.

"Good-night," I say, slowly spinning toward my door.

I stick the key into the lock and turn it. My heart is racing. Adrenaline is sprinting through my veins. I don't want the night to end, but I know it has to, and I know that this is its ending.

I turn back one last time and all at once feel a rebellious smile cross my face. He's just standing there with his perfect, muscle-laced body and his bright blue eyes, piercing my skin, and a crooked grin hanging on his lips. He's kind of exhilarating. I had forgotten what something like this feels like. It's kind of addicting. I kind of want more, but instead, I turn the knob, push through the door and close it gently behind me.

Once inside my little, dark apartment, I take a deep, excited breath and then hold back a sound that comes from somewhere deep inside my chest. In this moment, I don't feel guilty; I don't feel sad; I just feel...happy.

Chapter Thirteen

Patron Saint

"Okay, it's just about ready."

I turn off the light to the oven and search for a pot holder.

"Hey, you have Saint Michael."

I can hear his voice trailing off in the other room.

"What?" I ask.

"Saint Michael," Jorgen says. "Where did you get this?"

His question sounds purely curious, even though I don't have the slightest idea of what he's talking about yet.

I find the pot holder and pull it over my hand.

"Hmm?" I mumble.

I look up from the counter and notice him examining the pin that has sat on my bookshelf since I moved in. Instantly, I feel my heart sink a little deeper inside my chest.

"My sister," I say flatly, allowing my eyes to fall to the glove on my hand.

I'm not sure why I say I got it from Hannah. It just kind of comes out.

"Do you know who this is?" he asks.

I look up again. He's still examining the pin.

"Uh...Saint Michael?" I say, unsure, merely repeating his words.

I really don't know. It's a silver pin with a guy on it, and the guy has big wings, and I think he's carrying a sword. But that's all I know. I open the oven door and pull out a baking sheet.

"Come on," I say, "everything is almost ready."

"It's the patron saint of emergency technicians," he says, turning the pin over in his hand.

I laugh because I don't know what else to do, but it comes out sounding nothing like a laugh, as I feel my heart slam hard against the wall of my chest.

"Oh," I say, trying to sound unfazed.

I say the little word so softly I almost don't even hear it myself.

He's quiet for a minute. I fight back the warm tears welling up behind my eyelids before I even attempt to look up. But when I eventually do, his eyes fall into mine instantly—as if he's searching me. It feels as if he can read my soul. I quickly drop my gaze.

"Dinner is served," I say.

I feel him watching me for another moment before I look up and catch him setting the pin back down onto the shelf.

"I used to have one of those." He walks to the table, finds a chair and falls into it.

I continue to battle back the tears from the thoughts that shouldn't be there anymore. Thankfully, he doesn't seem to notice.

"I hope it's okay," I say, looking down at the two plates. "It's the only thing I really know how to make."

Jorgen looks down at his plate and back up at me.

"If it tastes as great as it looks, I'm in heaven."

"Okay, but just remember, I'm not the one who ever entertained the idea of becoming a chef."

"Hey," he says, "I entertained the idea. That's about as far as I got."

I laugh and take a seat next to him.

"Dinner was great. Way better than what I could have done."

I lower my eyes. "Thanks."

A silent moment passes between us. I really do hate silent, awkward moments, and my first instinct is to fill them as quickly as possible with the first thought that comes to my mind. "Do you have to go?"

He sets his eyes on mine but still offers no words.

"Or do you want to hang out and watch something?" I ask, hesitantly.

"Go?" His voice sounds surprised.

I hold my breath. I really don't want to scare him off by sounding desperate, but I do want him to stay. I'm learning that when he's around, I only think about him—about finding out who he is—and not about who I was or still am.

"There's nothing happening over there," he says, gesturing toward the door. "I'd much rather hang out here with you, if that's okay."

I say a thankful prayer and then fall into his blue eyes. I think it's the blue that helps me to feel at ease again.

"Food Network?" I ask, in an upbeat, but still shy, kind of voice.

"Just what I was thinking," he says.

Happy he wants to stay, I make my way to the couch and sit down on the far end of it. Jorgen follows me. I can tell he thinks about it before choosing a place near the middle.

I send him a playful, sideways grin after he sits down. He just smiles back at me. It's not what I was expecting, and it makes me nervous and giddy all at the same time.

I reach for the remote and punch in a few numbers. A reality cooking show is on. It's one of my favorites, but I just can't seem to shake the fact that this guy who was only a stranger a few weeks ago is now sitting just a couple feet from me on my couch. Every once in a while, I sneak a quick peek at him, and so far I've noticed that his dark hair has a natural wave to it, like it's almost curly; he has a strong five-o'clock shadow; he's got eyelashes a girl would kill to have; and a set a lips a girl would kill to kiss. And with all his dark features, his eyes look even bluer. I feel as if I'm not supposed to be noticing these things, but I just can't bring myself to stop.

"Do you want something to drink?"

I act as if I'm ungluing my eyes from a pure, uninterrupted stint of television watching and meet his gaze. "Uh, sure."

He gets up and makes his way into the kitchen. He seems curiously eager, so instead of offering to do the job myself, I just let him do it.

"There's tea in the fridge," I say.

I watch him stare at a set of cabinets, open them and then stare at another set.

"Next to the sink."

"Oh," he says, spinning around. "Got it."

He pulls out two glasses and pours some tea into each one. Then, he walks back into the living room.

"Thanks," I say, as he hands me a glass.

He takes a drink and then casually eyes up the couch again and eventually falls into a spot a foot closer to me than he had been before he ventured into the kitchen.

I narrow one eye, but he just simply returns my curious stare with a confident grin. It makes me laugh.

The show comes back on from a commercial break, and both our attentions go to the screen, until I hear his voice.

"You and Hannah are close?"

I look up at him. His eyes are planted on the photo of Hannah and me.

"Yeah, she's my best friend. She has her moments, but I decided a long time ago to keep her around regardless."

His eyes catch mine.

"That's nice," he says. "She's older, right?"

"Mm hmm." I nod my head. "Two years."

"Married?"

I nod my head again. "She married her college sweetheart."

There's a thoughtful look on his face now.

"What is the rest of your family like?"

"Well," I start, "they're all fairly sane, for the most part."

He studies me for a few seconds before a defiant smile pushes its way past my lips and he lowers his head and chuckles to himself.

"That's good," he says.

He looks back up a moment later, and I notice his eyes fall to a spot on my leg.

"That's one pretty crazy scar you've got there."

I follow his slow gaze to my shin. I know what he's talking about; I don't need to see it, so I don't know why I even bother looking. Maybe I had just hoped it would buy me some time.

My eyes eventually wander to his again. I can tell he's waiting for my response.

"Mm hmm," I say, nodding my head. "It's pretty crazy all right."

He tilts his head a little to one side. "I'm sure that one's got a story."

I take in a deep breath, then focus on one breath at a time.

"It does," I admit. "And it has a moral too: Don't do something stupid."

His face harbors a sober expression for a few long moments before he lowers his head.

I, meanwhile, let out a soft, uneasy exhale, happy that he seems to have chosen to leave it alone, at least for now.

"ACL surgery," he says.

I follow his fingers to the front of his knee.

"It's not as impressive as yours, but it's the biggest one I've got."

"How?" I ask.

"Playing football. Well, practicing," he adds. "I had a scholarship to a small school in Iowa, and I was doing a drill the summer before I was supposed to start."

"Gosh, that's awful. Did you lose your scholarship?"

"No. But I did lose my interest in playing football. By the time I was ready to go back, I had already decided

I wanted to be a paramedic, and I had been taking classes on the side. Plus, my knee really wasn't the same after that."

I lower my eyes before I lock gazes with him again.

"You don't ever wish you would have stayed?" I ask. "Tried to play, I mean."

He shakes his head.

"No." He seems to think about it for no more than a second. "I made the right decision at the time because at the time, I wanted it. I wanted to be a paramedic. I didn't want to risk my knee again. I didn't want to play scared—scared it'd tear again."

He pauses before he continues.

"I figure we've only got the present in front of us—that's all we've got to base a decision on. So, how can we go around faultin' ourselves for making a decision that's not based on what we want tomorrow? I can't tell you what I'll want tomorrow, and for all I know, I've only got today."

His blue eyes are fixed on mine when his lips stop moving, but I have no words. I don't know what to say.

My stare falls to the scar on my leg, and I can't help but think of the day I got it.

"Ada," I hear him say a moment later.

I force my attention back to him.

"You okay?"

I notice I'm all but frozen.

"I'm fine," I say.

His eyes burn into mine before he scoots closer and puts his arm around my shoulder. It doesn't feel weird because a hug seems like the best thing in the world right now. And he seems to know that—even though he can't possibly know just how breakable I really feel.

"The good news is that you win," he says, squeezing my body tighter into the muscles in his chest. His scent fills my lungs. It's almost intoxicating.

"What?" I ask.

"The scar contest. You have the biggest scar."

I laugh an unguarded laugh.

"What do I win?"

He doesn't say anything, so I turn my face up toward his, and after a moment, I notice his eyes leave a leisurely trail to my lips, and I quickly turn away, allowing a certain silence to sneak in between us. I don't even know how much time passes before I hear his voice again.

"Whatever your heart desires," he says, softly.

I slowly turn back toward him. He's smiling, and it's contagious.

"Hold me," I say.

My eyes meander back to the television, which has been pretty nonexistent until now, but all my attention stays wrapped up in him. I feel his muscular arms tighten around me, and then, I feel him pulling me down. I let him lower me to the couch and cradle me in his strong arms. And suddenly, I feel his coarse fingers lacing in mine until his hand all but engulfs my own. And in the next moment, his warm body is pressing against me, and I can feel his hard, broad chest rising and then falling in slow, rhythmic beats. It's exhilarating, and yet, all so strange—like a sobering reminder of what life feels like when all you feel is every touch—and nothing else.

Chapter Fourteen

Sleepover

I don't know how much time has passed when I wake up to a guy making pancakes on some show on TV. The light from the television is bright, and it forces my eyes shut. But when I feel warm breaths on my neck, my eyes shoot open again. And the first thing I notice is Jorgen's arm wrapped around my waist. Then, one by one, the details come rushing back to me. We talked for a long time after dinner about everything and nothing simultaneously—everything from our favorite holiday to our least favorite Smurf. His were Groundhog Day and Gargamel. And even after I pointed out that Gargamel wasn't a Smurf, he still picked Gargamel. I remember the silly conversations, but I don't remember falling asleep.

I lie as still as possible, while I try to plot out my next move in my head. He's still sleeping. I don't want to wake him, but I'm lying on my arm and it's completely asleep. And I'm not so sure I really want to be here when he wakes up either. It would be weird. Right? I barely know him. And what if he's weirded out? That would be even worse. And what if he smells my morning breath? Nope. That settles it. I've got to get out of here.

I carefully reach for my phone on the coffee table with the hand that's not fast asleep and press a button. All at once, its light fills the small space around us, and I panic and instinctively cover the screen with my other hand. *Oh Mylanta!* I'm screaming on the inside. A thousand tiny needles are suddenly stabbing my sleepy arm.

I grimace and lose a breath, but Jorgen doesn't stir. He seems to be unaffected by the light and my stabbing pain. I still don't move though, at least not until I can finally shift my arm without feeling the sharp tingles.

After about a minute, the pain is bearable, and I slowly lift my hand up a little and peek at the big numbers etched across my phone's screen. In a blinding, white glow, I read 2:30.

I clutch the phone in the palm of my hand and wait several seconds before carefully picking up his wrist with my two fingers and slowly sliding out from underneath his arm. His face shifts, and it stops me cold. I wait until he settles back into the throw pillow before I craftily stand up and turn back toward him to see if he's still asleep. He is, and he looks perfect—peaceful, manly, sexy, perfect—and it makes me want to crawl right back under his arm, but I don't. Instead, I grab the blanket at his feet, and I pull it to his shoulders and rest it gently against him. He is a beautiful creature. I wonder for a second how he got onto my couch, how he got into my life. I'm in awe of him in a way—in a way that I can't quite explain yet. I mean, besides the attractive part, which he's got down pretty well, he's got this way about him that makes me feel so comfortable around him even though I barely know him.

He shifts on the couch, and I instantly hold my breath as I watch him grab the blanket, settle deeper into the leather and gradually grow still again before my eyes catch the remote sitting on the coffee table. I quietly reach for it and turn off the TV. Then, I stand there for a good minute, maybe longer, trying to figure out if I really do need to go to my bed. I think about it—hard—before I finally decide I should. I take one last look at him and silently sigh. I'm already kicking myself for leaving him as I slowly tiptoe out of the living room and to my bedroom. In the dark, I shimmy off my clothes, throw on my sweatshirt and boxers, slide under the covers and close my eyes. Somehow, I just know I'm going to regret this in the morning.

My alarm clock nearly gives me a heart attack, just like it does every morning. I turn over and let my hand fall heavy onto its top button until it's quiet again.

It's another minute before I finally crack one eye open and probably another five before I throw back the covers and swing my legs over the side of the bed. Immediately, I feel the soft carpet under my bare toes, and one big yawn later, I'm on my feet.

My little apartment is draped in darkness, which doesn't really matter because my eyes are barely open anyway. Good thing my walk is only one straight stretch. *Ten. Eleven.*

I swing open the door, snatch up the morning paper and squeeze the rubber band off. The rubber band habitually slides onto my wrist as I open the newspaper to the last page. I shake the black and white sheets once to make them stiffen. Then, I swing around to the other side of the door and push my back against it until I hear it latch.

"Good morning, sunshine."

I drop the paper and let out a terrified, high-pitched scream. There's a man on my couch, and it takes me a second before I realize who it is.

"Jorgen," I finally say, once I've caught my breath. I'm literally panting as he sleepily sits up, wincing—no doubt from my Oscar-worthy scream.

"I didn't mean to scare you."

"No. I just...forgot you were here."

"Did we fall asleep?" he asks, rubbing his eyes.

"I think so." I reach down and pick up the paper.

"Did you...sleep here?" he asks, eyeing the couch.

I nod my head. "For a little while. But then I went to my room."

He looks kind of disappointed. "Well, I guess I better be gettin' home so you can get ready for work."

He stands up and walks over to me but then stops with only a foot between us. He's so close that I can smell his sweet cologne again.

"Last night was...," he says and then pauses, seeming to be searching for the right word.

"Nice," he finishes.

He opens the door but then slowly turns back toward me and steals a glance at me through hooded eyes. "That outfit really does look good on you."

I look down and notice my bare legs with the boxers nearly nonexistent. And instinctively, I roll my eyes and send him a playful smirk. But before I can even attempt anything resembling a comeback, he disappears behind the door, leaving me to my newspaper and my newfound giddy smile.

Chapter Fifteen

Leo

"So, what's Lucas doing tonight?"

Hannah looks at me and pushes her lips to one side, as if she's thinking.

"Video games; weird, scary movies; watching a rerun of some dumb, old football game—everything he can't do when I'm there," she says, sending me a devilish smirk.

"So, he's in heaven?" I ask.

She laughs. "Of course."

I plop down onto the couch with a big bowl of popcorn. "Okay, what are we watching?"

"Something really girly," Hannah suggests. "And preferably something with Leo."

"Oh, you know what?" I remember. "I just got *The Great Gatsby...*"

"No, you didn't," Hannah breaks in. She dramatically sighs and throws her hand to her heart. "I love Leo."

"I'll...take...that as a *yes* then."

I get up, grab the movie and feed it into the DVD player. Then, I plop right back down onto the couch with the popcorn.

"You know, when we were kids, I was convinced that I was going to marry him," Hannah says.

"You were also going to marry Prince William and one of the Hanson brothers too," I remind her.

She stops and seems to think about it. "Dang it. I was, wasn't I? What happened to me?"

I stare at her with knowing eyes.

"Lucas."

She looks up at me and then nods her head. "Lucas," she simply repeats, sighing happily to herself.

She grabs a handful of popcorn out of the bowl in my hands and shoves it into her mouth.

"Hey," she says, still chomping on the corn.

I barely even make out the word, her mouth is so full. It's a few seconds before she swallows and starts again.

"Do you remember that stupid game we made up when we were kids where we would pretend to sleep if someone came into a room?"

I start to laugh. "Yeah."

"How did that start anyway?"

"Mom," I say.

Hannah points her finger at me. "That's right!"

"She would call us to do something, and we would just act like we were sleeping. Evidently, you don't wake a sleeping kid."

106

Hannah bursts into laughter. "We got out of doing so much work with that. How did she never catch on?"

I shake my head. "How was she never concerned by how much we were sleeping all the time?"

Hannah stops laughing and squints her eyes in what looks like a thought. "You know, I have no idea."

She's quiet for a little too long, so I look over at her and catch her smiling to herself.

"That was such a stupid game," she adds.

I stuff a handful of popcorn into my mouth. "But it worked."

Snickering, she dramatically nods her head. "That it did."

"But, anyway," she goes on, shifting slightly on the couch, "the first time I met Lucas, I was a freshman in college, as you know, and I was at a friend's house. Lucas was there, but I had never met him before. He was the only person I didn't know out of like maybe six or seven of us sitting in the living room that night."

She stops and looks at me. "Have I ever told you this story?"

I start to shake my head. "Uh-uh, I don't think so."

"Okay," she goes on without missing a beat. "Anyway, Andie, one of my friends, was just about to walk into the room when Lucas all of a sudden whispers 'sleep.' And almost by instinct, my head goes down and I close my eyes."

All my attention darts to Hannah.

"No," I say. "There can't possibly be another soul in this world that knows the sleep game!"

"Well, he did," she says.

"You're kidding?" I think my jaw is stuck open.

"I know, right?" She laughs. "Everyone else just looked at us like we were crazy afterward. It's such a stupid, simple game. But he knew it."

She grabs another handful of popcorn. "I swear I fell in love with him right there." I watch her shake a finger at me. "There's always that moment when you just know you love someone."

Hannah's attention goes back to the screen then, while my mind travels back to Andrew and to a little dirt baseball field in the pouring rain. I had loved him before that day—even though I hadn't realized it. But in that moment, in the pouring rain, I knew there was no turning back.

A few minutes pass before the old memory eventually fades and my mind gets stuck on Lucas again. "I still can't believe he knew the sleep game."

It looks as if Hannah just barely gets her eyes to leave Leo and to venture back to mine.

"How?" I ask. "And how have you never told me that?"

"I don't know. I guess I just always forget. Evidently, he made it up too. I think one day he did it to get his little cousins to stop bothering him or something and then he found out it could work as an easy prank, and then, I guess it just kind of stuck."

"All this time, and I never knew." I think about it for another second and then cock my head to the side. "Hannah, he's like one of us."

"I know!" she squeals. "And we're such a rare, strange breed."

"Yeah," I say, still chewing my mouthful of popcorn. "I know."

"God," Hannah says, shaking her head. "We were a mess when we were kids."

"That. We. Were," I agree, drawing out every word for emphasis.

Hannah's quiet then, and so am I. Leo has returned to the screen, and instinctively, our eyes are glued to him again. But it's not long before Hannah breaks the silence.

"Hey, you remember when we tied James to that chair and left him under that old tree that one time?"

I almost spew my popcorn everywhere.

"He said he was Houdini." The little details come flooding back to me—as if it all happened just yesterday. "He said he could get out of anything."

"And he did get out of it," Hannah says, dramatically nodding her head.

"Yeah, like twelve hours later!" I swallow and start to laugh. "Do you remember that night? James came walking into Grandma's house right before dinner, and he was with Grandpa."

"Yeah, and he looked so terrified."

"Well, we had completely forgotten about him. It was dark, and he was only like seven. Wouldn't you have been terrified?"

Hannah lowers her eyes, and her shoulders rock forward. It looks as if she's trying not to laugh. "You know, Grandpa never said anything about it."

I think back to it for a second.

"You know what? He didn't," I remember. "But I do think he made some kind of deal with James though because you and I both know that James didn't get out of that chair alone."

"Hell, no, he didn't get out of it alone. I tied the knots! But what do you think the deal was?" she asks.

"I don't know, maybe like Grandpa would go along with James's story of him getting himself out of the chair if James wouldn't tell Grandma what had happened."

Hannah's hand flies to her mouth. "You know, that makes sense because even though James bragged about getting himself free later, neither he nor Grandpa ever said a word about it at dinner."

She pauses before she continues. "And plus, I guess Grandpa knew what he was doing. Remember when Grandma found out that James was our electric-fence tester?"

"Oh my gosh!" My hand instantly covers my heart. "I thought her eyes were going to pop right out of her head."

"I know! All I remember is that she was holding that big ball of bread dough. Remember? I know she thought about chucking it right at us." Hannah grabs another handful of popcorn and stuffs it into her mouth. "But it's not like we forced James to do it."

I almost choke on a kernel.

"Hannah, you said if he didn't do it, you'd tell everyone in the fifth grade that he used to wet his bed."

Hannah's eyes snap shut, and her narrow shoulders simultaneously jerk forward. "Oh, yeah."

I throw a piece of popcorn at her.

"Poor James," she adds, fishing the popcorn out of her hair.

I stare at her in amusement as she struggles to free the kernel from her long strands before my eyes slowly travel back to Leo on the screen. "Poor James," I agree.

"Good thing you were nice to him," Hannah says. I feel several popped kernels hit my head. "Or who knows how he would have turned out."

I shield myself from the flying corn. "Yeah, I totally claim his normalness."

We both look at each other then and laugh until our stomachs hurt because I think we both know that, based

110

on our wild childhood, there's not a good reason in this world as to why any one of us turned out fairly normal.

Chapter Sixteen

Eyes

"So, this is your place? It looks a lot like mine—just with different stuff."

Jorgen laughs. "Imagine that."

"I like it, though," I say, still looking around.

None of the furniture matches, but somehow it all fits together okay. And there's nothing on the walls really, except for a big, framed photo of the new Busch Stadium in the living room. Even it fits somehow.

"It's got this inspiring, bachelor pad kind of feel."

"Inspiring?" he asks.

My eyes continue to wander around the room, until they eventually catch on a tall lamp in the corner.

"Target?" I ask, gesturing toward the lamp.

He follows my stare to the corner.

"Yeah. How'd you know?"

I laugh to myself.

"I must be psychic."

He looks at me with two suspicious eyes.

"Or I have the same one in my bedroom," I confess.

He chuckles and hands me an envelope.

"You know, you could have just thrown this away. I'm pretty sure I'm not the millionth customer and the brand new owner of a..." I stop and read the front of the envelope. "A 2014 Lexus IS 350 Sport."

"Well, your name is on the envelope, and stealing someone's mail IS a federal offense these days. Plus, then I wouldn't have had a good excuse to get you over here to hang out with me."

I'm trying not to smile as I fall into the couch next to him. But when I look up, his eyes are already on me, and I just can't help it.

"You know," I say and then stop.

He tilts his head a little to the side.

"You have really pretty eyes. They're like the brightest blue I've ever seen in someone's eyes, but they're also kind of familiar in a strange kind of way."

He lowers his head. "Thanks, I guess."

I think I notice a little, bashful smile hanging on his lips.

"Does your sister have the same eyes?"

He sends me a questioning look.

"I don't know," I say in response to his look, "sometimes siblings share the same features—to where it's almost eerie, you know?"

"Eerie?"

His forehead fills with little wrinkles.

"Yes, eerie," I confirm with a laugh.

He shakes his head.

"No, she has green eyes—kind of like yours."

I take a second and push my lips to one side. "Hmm."

"That's her in that photo up there," he says.

My eyes follow his gesture toward the entertainment center where a small photo leans up against a couple of DVD cases. I get up and make my way over to it.

"She's really pretty. What's her name?"

I glance back at him. He's propping his feet up onto his coffee table now.

"Lindsey," he says.

I inspect the image a little more. "You guys have the same nose."

"Really?" he asks, as if he's never noticed.

"Yeah, if I didn't already know you two were related, I'd guess it by your noses."

I set the photo back down.

"What about you and Hannah? You guys don't look much alike."

"We have the same eyebrows."

"Eyebrows?"

He asks it with so much disbelief that it makes me laugh. "I'm not kidding," I say.

He stares at the space between my forehead and my eyes now. "How can anyone have the same eyebrows?"

I really try not to laugh, so he knows I'm serious, but in the end, I'm not very successful at it.

"Just look next time you see her. I promise," I say, joining him on the couch again.

He nods his head, chuckling to himself. "Okay."

I grab a throw pillow and squeeze it to my chest. I'm really surprised he even has a throw pillow until I feel something furry protruding from it. I quickly flip it around and notice there's a bear on the other side with half of its body sticking out of the pillow. I slowly turn the pillow so that the bear is facing Jorgen.

He notices it and simply shrugs his shoulders. "I'm a hell of a decorator?"

My eyes playfully narrow on him.

"No?" he says.

I shake my head.

"Okay, my mom and dad went to Colorado a few years back. It's a souvenir."

I nod my head in satisfaction.

"Better," I say.

The room is quiet then as my eyes fall to the bear in the pillow again. What a strange, little pillow. I squeeze it to my chest and look back up at Jorgen when a thought crosses my mind.

"Jorgen."

"Hmm?" he asks.

"What's your middle name?"

He just stares at me with no expression written on his face whatsoever, and after a moment, he shakes his head. "Nah," he says.

I feel my face crumpling in confusion, but I'm also trying to hold back a laugh. He looks so serious all of a sudden. "What?"

"Nah," he says again, still shaking his head.

He runs his hand through his hair and then his palm down his thigh as if he's nervous or something.

"What? Come on. You know mine."

"Yours is a good one, though."

"Jorgen, it can't be that bad."

He just gives me the most serious stare down I've ever seen, but it only makes me laugh.

"Jorgen," I scold playfully.

His stoic features don't budge.

"Okay, if I can guess it, you'll confirm it, right?"

"You'll never guess it."

"First letter," I say.

He seems to think about it for a second, as if he's not even sure he wants to give that much away.

"Fine," he pouts. "*F.*"

"*F?*"

He nods his head.

"Okay. Frank?"

"No," he says.

"Ferdinand?" I guess again.

He shakes his head. "No."

"Fffffido?"

"What?" He laughs. "Like the dog?"

It's the first smile from him in nearly a minute.

"Well, I can't think of any more names that start with F. Come on, Jorgen, just tell me."

He closes his eyes and then mumbles something under a heavy breath.

I tilt my head to the side. "What was that?"

"Felix," he says, a little louder this time.

"Felix?" I ask. "Like the cat?"

His eyes dart to mine, and at last, a grin pushes past his lips. "Like the cat," he confirms, lowering his eyes and looking defeated.

I throw the bear-pillow his way. It hits his arm and falls into his lap. I watch him retrieve it and then slowly look back up at me through hooded eyes.

"I like it," I say.

"You have to say that."

"What? Why do I *have* to say that?"

"Because you're nice, and I'm sitting right here," he explains.

116

"Not true," I say. "Even if I were mean, and you were sitting millions of miles away from me on some couch holding a bear-pillow on Pluto, I would still like it. It's a very strong name. It fits you," I add.

I watch a smile slowly start to edge its way across his tan face, and before I know it, I'm stuck in his eyes again.

"What?" he asks, after a few moments of my staring.

"It's nothing," I say. "They're just so unique, but so familiar."

"My eyes?"

"Mm hmm," I confirm.

He looks down, and his big eyelashes seem to rest on his cheeks for a moment before he locks gazes with me again.

"Well, maybe we knew each other in another life," he offers.

I lower my head and gently laugh, until I feel his hand on my chin. He lifts my face until my eyes are even with his.

"Or maybe we were just meant to find each other in this one," he says, smiling softly.

My heart breaks a little. I want to believe him.

Then, suddenly, I'm aware of my every breath and his too, as each falls one by one onto my lips. I close my eyes. I want to give in, but instead, I panic.

"Or maybe we shared an alley in our cat lives," I push out, opening my eyes again.

Jorgen's gaze falls from mine, but it returns only moments later.

"That's probably it," he says, softly chuckling to himself.

I laugh too, but mine is a nervous one. I pray he doesn't notice.

"Come here," he says, pulling me closer to him.

I let him put his arm around me and rest his hand on my thigh. Then, I lean into him and lay my head gently onto his chest, and instantly, I can feel his heart beating. I'm still not sure how I fit into this new life yet. I'm still trying to figure it all out as fast as I can without falling to pieces in the process, but I also don't know how much longer I can resist this beautiful creature beside me.

Chapter Seventeen

Moving

"Lada, have you ever thought about moving? You know, just picking up and starting over?"

I stare right at Hannah. She's kidding. Right? How does she not know that I'll never be in the mood to have this conversation with her?

"Well, have you?" she asks again.

I continue to glare at her, willing her to drop it. Of course, I've thought about picking up and starting over. I thought about it once right before college, four years ago, but it hurt so much that I pushed it away and never thought about it again.

"Why?"

"What do you mean *why*?" she asks.

I look at her with a straight face, daring her to say it.

"I don't know," she says instead. "There's so much here. Don't you ever get tired of seeing it—reliving it?"

I stuff a towel into my bag.

"I'm fine, Hannah."

"Okay, okay. I was just asking."

I roll my eyes and fling open the door.

Jorgen is at his door fiddling with his keys. He's wearing his navy pants, white collared shirt and work boots. He stops for a second and looks up at me.

I smile because that's what I do around him now.

"Work?" I ask.

He nods his head.

"Pool?" he asks.

I nod my head.

"Food Network tomorrow night?" he asks.

I nod my head again.

"Have fun at the pool," he calls back at me as he makes his way down the stairs.

"Have fun at work," I call down to him.

When he's gone, I find Hannah lurking in my personal space behind me. Her eyes are big and staring straight through me.

I crinkle my eyebrows at her.

"You're in my bubble," I say, frowning and chalking off an imaginary circle around me.

"You like him, don't you?" Hannah scolds, crossing her arms at her chest.

Despite her demeanor, I can tell she's excited. I don't say anything. I just walk out the door.

"Do you guys hang out?"

"We're just friends, Hannah."

"Mm hmm," she says.

I know she doesn't believe me.

We walk the rest of the way in silence. And when we get past the gates, we find two lounge chairs side by side. Hannah lays down her towel and takes a seat in one. I do the same and take a seat in the one next to it. She pulls a magazine out of her bag. I find a book in mine, pull it out and start reading. But no sooner do I get past the first page, Hannah fumbles her magazine and sighs.

"Lada, he's gorgeous, you know. I mean his arm muscles are as big as my..."

She stops and looks at her bikini-clad body.

"As my thighs," she finishes.

I look at her thighs.

Hannah was never really good with comparisons or proportions, for that matter.

"Gosh, now I can see why you don't even want to think about moving," she adds.

I glare at her again. She doesn't seem to notice. She's facing straight into the sun now—eyes closed, her big sunglasses threatening to swallow her face. I helped her pick them out. They didn't look so big in the store.

Then, all of a sudden, she makes a rash movement in my direction, and just like that, she's on her side and staring at me.

"Has he kissed you?"

She dramatically lifts her big shades from her eyes.

"What?" I ask, starting to laugh.

"Has he kissed you?" she asks again.

"No, Hannah."

"Well, are you dating?"

"I don't know...No," I say.

"Has he come over?"

She continues her rapid-fire questioning.

"Yes," I say.

Her eyes grow wide.

"Lada," she squeals, shoving my arm.

She grabs my thick, dark hair next and gently runs it through her fingers.

"You guys would make the prettiest babies," she says, before she sets her sunglasses back onto her nose and positions her back flat against the chair again.

"Hannah," I scold.

It doesn't faze her, so I give up and return my attention to my book. But I get exactly two lines read, and I hear her voice again.

"Then when it seems we will never smile again, life comes back."

I close the book and face her.

"Did you just make that up?"

"No," she says, laughing. "Mark M. Baldwin did."

I set my face toward the sun again, and I think about my old life—the one I feel as though I've abandoned somehow. It hurts to think of it that way. And even though I know it wasn't perfect, I look back now, and all I see is perfection. Every soft whisper, every spoken word, every gentle touch—it's all perfect. Time won't let me see it otherwise. They're all just perfect memories— perfect, untouchable moments that came and went so softly that they almost feel as if they were always just a dream.

"Hannah."

My voice is soft and thoughtful now as I wait for her attention to shift back to me.

"I'm scared it'll never be the same with anyone else," I confess.

She slowly shakes her head. "No," she admits, "it won't."

A breath lifts my chest and then a sigh lowers it again, even though I expected her response. I expected it because I already know it won't be. I already know that no matter what, it will never be the same.

"It'll be different," she goes on. "But different isn't always bad."

I meet her eyes behind her big shades. Then, I return to the sun and let its heated rays wash over me.

"Lada," I hear her say a second later.

My face turns toward hers again.

"I'm happy for you."

I smile at her because I know she means it.

"We're just friends," I say.

"I know. But I'm still happy."

She says her last words and then goes back to getting her suntan. And suddenly, I feel my smile edging a little higher up my face and a soft tingle coming to life in my chest—and all I can think is that it's because I'm starting to feel happy too.

Chapter Eighteen

Hope

"Lada, I had an extra coupon for that toothpaste you like, so I picked you up a tube," Hannah says, charging into my apartment.

She stops when she sees Jorgen in the living room.

"Oh...hi," she stutters apologetically. "I'm sorry; I didn't know Lada had company."

Jorgen laughs. "It's fine. How are you, Hannah?"

Hannah looks as if she's trying not to blush. She still turns into a thirteen-year-old, smitten school girl around guys that look like Jorgen. I'm not much better sometimes, but she's definitely worse.

"Great," she says and then absentmindedly sets the tube onto the counter.

I reach over the sink in the kitchen and pick up the toothpaste. "Thanks, Hannah."

She looks as if she tries to respond to me, but instead uses all her efforts to fall gracefully into one of my barstools. I, meanwhile, catch Jorgen pointing to his eyebrow, eyeing Hannah and miming the word *same*. He has this goofy, surprised look on his face. I quickly lower my eyes and try to hold in a laugh, and I think Hannah notices.

"So, what are you two up to?" she asks.

I look up at Jorgen again. He's still wearing that goofy grin.

"Nothing," we both say, almost simultaneously.

Hannah sends me a suspicious look.

"No, seriously, we both just got off work," I say.

She nods her head and pushes her lips together, seemingly satisfied.

"Oh!" she suddenly exclaims. "Lada, remember that book I said I wanted to borrow of yours—that one about the guy from Missouri. Can I borrow it?"

"Uh, sure, it's on the shelf over there." I gesture toward the living room. "Jorgen, can you grab it for her. It's the one on the end with the tan-ish cover."

Jorgen examines the shelf for a second and then slides a book toward him, sending something falling to the floor.

It catches Hannah's attention, and I watch her face quickly turn curious as Jorgen reaches down to pick up the object.

"You still have that thing?" Hannah asks.

I look at what's now in Jorgen's hand.

"Hannah," I whisper, trying to get her attention.

It doesn't work, and she continues.

"We call that Lada's hope," Hannah says, gesturing with her eyes toward Jorgen's hands.

Jorgen looks at the book.

"The pin," Hannah clarifies. "Of Saint Michael."

I watch as Jorgen's eyes travel back to the pin in his hand, and I think that Hannah's done.

"We have no idea where she got it from," Hannah goes on. "It was just there that day."

I freeze. I literally stop moving, breathing, all of it. In exactly five seconds flat, my mouth has gone completely dry, my mind has flashed to a blank canvas and I have lost every single one of my words—Every. Single. One. I wait for Jorgen's eyes to find mine. They do only seconds later. He looks slightly confused.

Hannah doesn't say anything else, and I'm more than thankful. At least she stopped at that. At least she spared him my whole life story. I'm still going to kill her, but at least she stopped before Jorgen had to witness it.

Silent moments pass, and I'm pretty sure just enough go by to make it awkward. I can feel Jorgen's eyes still on me, while my own gaze has fallen to the pin in his hand.

"Well...I...just wanted to drop off the tooth...paste," I hear a small voice utter.

For the first time in almost a minute, I notice that Hannah is still in the room.

"I...should get going. Lada, call me later."

I stare straight through her then as she backs away from me and toward Jorgen. I know she realizes she has said too much.

"It was nice seeing you again, Jorgen," Hannah says, sliding the book out of his hand.

Jorgen seems to snap out of a trance just in time to acknowledge Hannah, and then Hannah's gone, and it's only Jorgen and I left in the room.

I take a breath and let go of a sigh.

"Okay," I say, "so Hannah didn't give the pin to me. Someone else did, but I don't know who it was. And it was a long time ago."

He's staring at me when I finish, and he seems pale and a little like he still doesn't fully believe me.

I feel really stupid for lying to him in the first place. I feel even more stupid after having been caught in the stupid lie. But I feel bad too because I know I've skirted the truth yet again. There's more to the story, even though I really don't remember exactly how I got the pin. Like Hannah's big mouth said, it was just there. But the thing is, I've only known Jorgen for a little more than a month now. I'm just not ready to tell him the whole story.

My stare catches on the empty counter before I meet his eyes again. They still look off somehow.

"Jorgen?"

"Yeah," he says quietly, setting the pin back in its place on the shelf.

"Are you okay?" I ask.

He makes his way over to me without saying a word, then stops right in front of me.

"What?" I whisper.

He doesn't seem mad or weirded out, but I feel as if he should—at least a little. I did lie to him.

In the next second, his arms are around me, and he's squeezing me into his body. My mind races, and I try to figure out exactly what's going on before I just give in and slowly wrap my arms around him too. I hold him tight, inhale the sweet smell of his cologne and press my hands flat against the muscles in his back. I feel as if I'm literally melting into his embrace when I hear him whisper into my hair.

"Will you come home with me?"

He pulls away from me and holds my shoulders in the palms of his hands.

"Across the hall?" I ask, timidly.

He laughs once and then slowly shakes his head.

"No, home," he says. "The county fair's next week. Will you come with me?"

I search his eyes until I feel genuine excitement coming to life on my face.

"Okay," I agree.

He gives me this look then, as if he's waiting for me to change my mind or something.

"Really?" he asks.

I nod my head and start to laugh. "Yeah," I confirm.

A wide grin lights up his face, and then he pulls me into his arms again.

I'm not completely sure what I've just agreed to. It sounds awfully close to something you'd do if you were in a relationship. And though I'm not completely opposed to the idea, I'm pretty sure a real relationship with Jorgen Ryker or anyone new, for that matter, is next to impossible in my situation.

Jorgen leaves, and I find myself gravitating toward the pin on the shelf. I pick it up and caress its indented surface with my fingertips. I don't keep anything from my old life where I can see it, but I do keep this out. Hannah was right. It was my hope; it is my hope. I didn't think of it that way at all when I first had it in my hand. But now, looking back, it really was my hope—my tiny glimmer of hope—like something was telling me to keep going, to keep fighting, to fight back, to live. And now, I think, it's kind of become like a testament to human survival for me—like it reminds me of just how strong we really can be when we have to be and that just when we think we can't possibly go on, we do.

Chapter Nineteen

'64 Ford

"Damn train," I hear him mumble under his breath as he pulls to the side of the two-lane road.

I look up to see a train frozen and stretched across the part of the tracks where the truck is supposed to drive across.

"Okay, we'll have to get out here."

He smiles his crooked smile at me and then pushes open his door. I watch him climb out and shut the door behind him. And after a second, I follow his lead and do the same, even though I'm now one-part bewildered and one-part amused.

"I don't know why the damn thing stops here like this all the time."

He's talking to me but not talking to me at the same time.

"I live on the other side of these tracks. Are you up for a little walk?"

I know my expression turns curious—fast. I'm not exactly sure what I've signed up for yet, but at least now I'm happy that I chose to wear my comfortable boat shoes earlier this morning instead of something less forgiving on my feet.

"When you say 'walk,' are we talking down the block or more like a day's journey?"

I can see in between the railcars, and there's a shed and a little, winding stretch of highway, but other than that, it's all flat fields and nothing much else for miles.

"There's an old truck in that shed over there," he says, pointing at a spot behind the cars. "It's there mostly for times like this."

I watch lines form near the corners of his eyes as he holds out his hand. And I can't help but smile too when I lay my fingers against his.

He swings his legs over the labyrinth of metal and chains that connects the two train cars next and then turns back toward me.

"I know this is pretty much after the fact, but this is safe, right?" I ask.

A playful expression dances to his face.

"It is until it starts movin'."

I feel my eyes growing wide right before I scurry up onto the metal hitch, steady myself with the help of Jorgen's hand and then quickly jump off. Immediately, I feel my feet hit the loose gravel on the other side of the tracks, and I let go of a thankful breath.

"You okay?" he asks.

"Yeah," I say, securing a strand of my hair behind my ear with my free hand. "There's really no other way in?"

He slowly shakes his head back and forth. "Not from this side."

"How often does it just stop here like this?"

"Oh, about once a month or so," he says casually, as if it's just another fact of life.

The way he says it makes me laugh.

"Come on," he says, setting out down the black asphalt with my hand still in his.

The asphalt is the only thing, once we cross the tracks, that reminds me that I'm still in the twenty-first century. I mean, I'm not exactly from the most bustling of metropolises either, but we do have grocery stores and hospitals...and lines on our roads. My eyes fixate on the black highway that carves a winding path through corn fields for several miles. There's not a single white or yellow mark on it.

"So, this is home?"

He angles his face my way. He's wearing a happy, boyish grin, and I can't help but notice there's a new spark in his eyes all of a sudden.

"This is home," he confirms.

It's about a quarter of a mile to the shed. We reach it about five minutes later and make our way to one side where there's a big door made of wooden slats. We stop at it, and Jorgen reaches up and lifts a latch, then pulls the door open.

"Watch your step," he says, holding out his hand.

I lay my hand in his again before I look down and step over the raised, wooden ledge and onto the dirt floor.

It's dark inside the shed. There are no windows, but the sun pouring in from the open door lends me just enough light to see that there's a thick, gray tarp covering something big in front of us.

I watch as Jorgen bends down at one of the corners of the tarp and starts pulling it up. He pulls it up and then over and then gathers it into his arms.

"Ol' Red," he announces, once he's got the tarp squished into a big ball.

He gestures toward an old truck painted a bright cherry red.

"What year is it?"

I can't believe something that looks this old still runs.

"It's a '64."

I walk around the front of it. There's a clear bug shield running the width of the hood. The words *Ol' Red* are written on it in black, cursive stenciling.

"It really is Ol' Red," I say, pointing to the letters.

"Sure is," he says, smiling back at me.

I take another good look at the old truck. "I love it," I say and mean it.

I watch Jorgen walk to the back of the shed and swing open two big wooden doors. Dust goes flying every which way. I can see its particles hanging on the sun's rays, though Jorgen doesn't seem to notice it so much.

He walks over to the passenger's door then and pulls on it. It comes open but not without a noisy squeak.

I peer into the cab. Inside, the seats are vinyl, and the same cherry red as what's on the outside of the truck covers the inside too, including the dashboard. And there's a big steering wheel on the driver's side made wholly out of metal with what looks like a small doorknob fastened to it.

I climb onto the seat, and Jorgen gently closes the door but then gives it a good, forceful push until it latches. Inside the cab, I notice there's a long shifter coming out of the floor and only two little metal knobs for the radio. Out of pure habit, I reach for my seatbelt, but I don't feel anything. I look above my shoulder and notice the reason why I don't feel one is because there isn't one.

Jorgen hops in behind the wheel a minute later, and immediately, my eyes fall on him. I watch him reach up above his head and pull down the visor. A keychain with one key attached to it falls to his lap.

"Theft not so bad here, I guess?"

He looks at me with a wide grin.

"Not so bad," he confirms.

He sticks the key into the ignition and purrs the engine to a start before backing out of the shed and onto the little dirt path that leads to the blacktop. From the big side mirror, I can see the dust trail that's left in our wake.

So far, this trip has yielded a string of firsts for me—my first train hopping, my first ride in Ol' Red, my first look into Jorgen Ryker's life. It's making me want to stop and stay awhile—even if it is just to see what this sexy creature beside me is all about.

I use the metal lever on the door to roll down my window. The glass seems to come down in two-inch increments and is all the way down in no time. I stare out the window then and let the warm wind pouring through it hit my skin and toss strands of my hair around my face. The dusty trail still hovers over the dirt path in the side mirror. And the train is still frozen on the tracks. We drive parallel to it for a little while longer, until we take a slight bend in the road and start heading away from it. The turn of the wheel makes an object dangling from the rearview mirror sway slightly to one side. It catches my eye and soon, curiosity claims me.

"What is that?"

Jorgen glances at me and then follows my stare to the mirror before he laughs gently and then sets his eyes back on the road again.

"It's my dad's tassel. This was his first car."

The tassel is a faded red and yellowed white with the number *81* in tarnished silver at the top.

I watch the tassel sway back and forth for a moment before I return my attention to Jorgen. His eyes are still planted on the road. One arm is resting on the ledge of the open window; one hand is barely on the big steering wheel. He looks so comfortable—as if he fits perfectly inside a 1960-something truck with the words *Ol' Red* painted across the bug shield. The thought makes me laugh inside, until I catch his finger lift up from the steering wheel, and I'm distracted again. There's another much newer truck coming at us. I watch as the driver of the newer truck lifts a finger as he passes, and I can't help but laugh out loud this time.

"Was that a wave?"

He sends a questioning look my way. "Yeah," he says, before he plants his eyes back on the road.

"Who was it?"

He glances across the cab at me, still smiling, and then shrugs his shoulders.

"You don't know him? But you just waved at him," I say.

Suddenly, he beams. "It's how you tell the insiders from the outsiders, baby. Welcome to the river bottoms."

Baby? All of a sudden, he has this new air of confidence about him or maybe it's more like comfort— the kind that makes *baby* sound so perfectly normal and also so perfectly sexy. There's a happy, tingly feeling in my chest, but I also feel my eyebrows slightly furrowing.

"The insiders wave...," I start.

"The outsiders don't," he finishes.

"Aah," I say, allowing my head to fall gently against the back window. "I know all your secrets now, Jorgen Ryker."

He just smiles. "Just about."

It's another mile on the blacktop before Ol' Red climbs a levee and then wanders down a gravel road. It's flat on the other side of the levee too, with more fields for miles and only a few houses in view. And one house, in the far-off distance, even looks as if it might be abandoned. Its outside is gray and through its windows, all I can see is a dark and sleepy inside.

We finally get to a long, white-graveled driveway, turn into it and eventually stop in front of a two-story farmhouse. It's made of wood and painted white, and I think it still has a tin roof.

Jorgen gets out and then jerks open my door. It squeaks again but not nearly as bad as the first time.

"They're all probably inside," Jorgen says, helping me out of the truck.

"They?" I try to ask without sounding terrified.

"Oh, don't worry, it's just my mom and my grandma. I've just got to run in for a second. You wanna come?"

"Of...course," I stutter. Of course *home* would mean meeting his family. I don't know why that never crossed my mind. I silently put myself back together. I can do this. I meet new people every day in my job. I tell myself it's just like that as I tug at the bottom of my tank top and try to brush out my wind-blown hair with my fingers.

I follow Jorgen up three concrete stairs to a little porch lined with hanging baskets full of bright red flowers.

"Mom, we're here." Jorgen pushes through a screen door.

There's a room to the left; stairs in front of us; and a hallway to the right. We go right, and I follow Jorgen down the hallway, but an open door to a den-like room suddenly makes me stop. Hanging on the wall, there's a framed newspaper clipping of the same photo I uncovered of him standing next to the cow. I stop and stare at it. Underneath the frame is another photo. It's of his sister. She's wearing a crown and a sash.

"What'd you find?"

Jorgen's facing me again.

"I just...Is that you?" I feign ignorance, point to the frame and wait for him to walk back to me.

When he sees the photo, he lowers his head and chuckles, then walks into the room.

"That would be me." He examines the photo more closely. "All one hundred pounds of me."

I laugh and join him in the room.

"And that's Lindsey?" I ask.

His eyes fall to the frame.

"Yeah. She was homecoming queen her senior year. You wouldn't know it by this picture, but she hated every moment of it."

I cock my head to the side.

"Lindsey's not really the girly type," he says. "And I think that's why she won. Everyone knew that."

I laugh again, but this time, my eyes catch another photo on the opposite wall.

"Wait, who is that?"

I walk closer to the other frame.

"Jorgen, is this you?"

There's a little kid in the photo. He's maybe four, and he's holding a fish that's almost his size.

"Yeah, my first catfish."

"Is that your dad?" I point to a man in waders helping to hold up the fish.

"Yeah, I think he was more excited than I was. Don't let him fool ya; he's a sentimental old fart."

I stare at the photo some more and then glance back at Jorgen. "You were cute."

"Were?" he asks. He's wearing a sideways smirk, and it's as sexy as hell.

I playfully roll my eyes. *If he only knew.*

He walks closer to me and takes my hand.

"Jorgen, was that you?" A woman's voice echoes through the hallway, but for a moment, it does little to faze Jorgen.

His stare lingers in mine, and all I can think about is kissing him. When I'm not lost in his eyes, I can make up all the excuses in the world for why I shouldn't just devour those prefect lips of his. But in those eyes...it's a whole different ball game.

"We should probably go say 'hi' before she convinces herself she's hearin' things and checks herself into the loony bin too soon."

"Yeah," I agree, slowly nodding my head. "We should."

I don't really agree, simply because I want to stay in his eyes, but I follow him out of the room and down the narrow hall anyway.

The floors are wooden, and they creak with each step. But with each step, I'm also a little more excited. I know I'm still nervous for some reason because I still keep trying to brush out my hair, but at the same time, I

138

also can't wait to find out more about this man, whose stare and lips have taken over my mind.

We get to the end of the hallway, and suddenly, there's an overwhelming smell of apples and cinnamon.

"Jorgen!" I hear a woman exclaim.

Jorgen hugs the woman and then goes to hug a shorter, older woman with gray hair.

"And you must be Ada."

The younger of the two women closes in on me and instantly throws her arms around my shoulders.

"Hi," I say, as she squeezes me tight.

The woman pulls away and then goes to brushing off one of my shoulders.

"Oh, I'm sorry, dear. I'm covered in flour. We're baking for the church picnic tomorrow. That's why I don't have a sit-down dinner. But I did whip up a salad, and there's some pasta that Grandma made in the Crock-Pot."

She points to a table in the center of the room.

"Mom," Jorgen says, "it's fine. We're just stopping by. We're headed to the fair."

"Hogwash," the older woman chimes in. "You can't feed this beautiful girl candy apples and popcorn for dinner."

The old woman ambles over to me and takes my hand with both of hers.

"Hi, dear, you'll stay and eat something before you go, won't you?"

I look up at Jorgen. His eyes are already on mine as if he's waiting for my response. I send him a smile to let him know it's okay with me.

"All right," he says. "But she's got to save room for dessert. So, no tempting us with any of whatever you got back there." Jorgen gestures toward a counter lined with baked goods.

"Oh, we won't," the older woman says, squeezing my hand, and at the same time, giving me a sly wink.

I try to hold in a laugh. Something tells me this woman was a force to be reckoned with before her first gray hair.

Jorgen and I sit down at the little table, and Jorgen fills my plate, and we eat and listen to the older woman talk about the key to a perfect pie crust, which somehow involves keeping the men out of the kitchen. And every once in a while, Jorgen's mom finds an open space in the conversation to ask about me and what I do and where I'm from, but I get the hint that she already knows all the answers. She reminds me a lot of my mom. She seems gentle on the outside but also like one of those people, who, if you pulled back a layer, all you'd find was pure strength and determination.

"Oh, and Jorgen, your dad and grandpa finally found your old toy riding tractor. How on earth did it get to that old house on the Steelman's place?"

Jorgen almost chokes on his salad. "I completely forgot about that."

His mom is staring at him now, presumably waiting for his answer.

Jorgen swallows and then moves his head back and forth a little, as if he's trying to play it off. "Lindsey and I threw it on the back of the five-wheeler one day and took it over there."

His mom doesn't look satisfied, and Jorgen seems to notice that.

"Okay," he huffs. "We put a piece of plywood on the steps and took turns ridin' down it."

I force myself not to laugh as the woman instantly tosses her hand to her heart and shakes her head.

"I swear, I'm not asking any more questions. I don't even want to know how many times you kids could have killed yourselves growing up."

"They were kids, Diane," the older woman chimes in. "They survived. You don't want me to get started on half the shenanigans you and your sister put me and your father through when you were little."

Jorgen's mom hardly bats an eye at the older woman, but she does smile at me before she goes back to kneading her dough. I can only guess that smile confirms the truth in the old woman's words.

"Why were they lookin' for that old thing anyway?" Jorgen asks.

His mom pats the dough and then lets out a breath. "Oh, they want to 'restore' it." She uses her fingers to make quotation marks. "You know, paint it, oil it, whatever they do."

"A toy tractor?" Jorgen asks.

"Well, it was yours when you were little," she says, bringing a plate of brownies to the table and setting them down in front of us. Jorgen takes the plate and pushes it aside.

"We're getting dessert at the fair," he whispers to me.

He winks then, and I just smile to myself.

"So, why are they fixin' it up again?" Jorgen asks.

His mom stops and touches his shoulder. "They'll never admit it, but they miss it sometimes."

"It?" he questions.

"You'll understand when your kids are grown someday, dear." She walks back to her station behind the counter. "God knows your father and grandfather didn't worry half as much as I did about just getting you and your sister to adulthood in one piece."

Jorgen narrows one eye at me, and I just snicker. I'm beginning to see that our childhoods really weren't that much different.

We finish our meals a few minutes later, and Jorgen takes my plate.

"Mom, where's Dad?"

"We sent him outside," the older woman puffs.

Jorgen looks at me and then at his mom. "Okay, well, we're going to take off so we can get there before they shut the fair down."

We say our goodbyes and then head out a back door off a little room attached to the kitchen.

"Dad." I hear Jorgen say before we're even out the door. "Truck's in town. Can I borrow yours?"

"Sure, Son." The man squeezes Jorgen's arm but continues toward me.

"Victor," the man says.

"Ada," I say, meeting his outstretched hand.

"Well, now I can finally say that I've met someone famous."

My eyes dart to Jorgen. He just smiles, and I shake my head.

"And Son, you didn't warn me of how pretty she is."

My smile quickly turns bashful, and heat rushes to my cheeks. I pray that I don't turn beet red right in front of him.

I manage to find Jorgen's stare again through my hooded eyes. It's locked on mine, and for the first time, I notice a certain softness in his eyes that I don't think I've ever noticed before.

"You meet Grandpa yet?" Jorgen's dad asks me.

I start to shake my head. "No, not yet."

"Where is he?" Jorgen asks.

"In his rocking chair," his dad says.

Jorgen takes my hand. "Okay, we'll head over there. But then, we're takin' off."

"Ada, it was so nice to meet you."

I smile at his dad and then feel Jorgen tugging me along toward a big, unattached shed or garage or something. Its bay doors are open, and the first thing I see is a little, old man sitting in a green, wooden rocking chair.

"Ada, this is my Grandpa E," Jorgen says, gesturing toward the aged man.

"Hi," I say. "Nice to meet you."

"No, no, dear, the pleasure's all mine," the old man says with a sweet smile.

"Grandpa E, how's it going?" another younger voice calls out from behind us.

"Still vertical," Grandpa E shouts over his shoulder and then goes back to his rocking.

"Did those women kick you out of the house again?" the younger man asks.

"No, I left on my own accord." The old man chuckles to himself.

The younger man laughs too and then sets his eyes on Jorgen and me.

"Hi," he says, planting his feet in front of me. "Marcus."

He holds out his hand, and I habitually place my hand in his.

"Ada," I say.

"Ada, this is the buddy that plays on the softball team I think I mentioned before," Jorgen says.

I take a second, remembering.

"Oh, yeah," I say, starting to nod my head. "How are you guys doing?"

Marcus immediately lowers his head.

"Well, we're 2 and 4, but I think we're still all trying to get used to playin' with each other, you know? We've got a bunch of these newbies, and Jorgen over here up and left us."

He stops then and puts a finger to his chin.

"Hell," Marcus goes on, "I think Jorgen has been here the two times we've actually won this season."

He raises an eyebrow at me.

"Maybe you could convince him to get back here for our next game," he says, sending me a wink.

I laugh and find Jorgen's stare, already on me.

"I'll see what I can do," I say.

Jorgen smiles at me and then turns his attention to Marcus. "So, what are you up to?"

"Oh, I've got a tree that was hit by lightning a while back. I'm finally gettin' around to cuttin' it down, and I'm borrowin' your dad's chainsaw."

"Aah," Jorgen says, rocking back on his heels and catching my gaze again.

"So, you guys going to the fair tonight?"

I hear Marcus's voice, but everything else about me is stuck on Jorgen's stare.

"Yeah," Jorgen eventually says, making sure to keep his eyes on mine. "We're headed out there now."

"Okay," I hear Marcus say in the background. "I'll see you out there then."

I press my lips together and finally lower my eyes. He's killing me. He has to know that with those eyes and that forever crooked smile of his, he's irresistible. Any other guy, I don't think I'd be here right now. In fact, I know I wouldn't be here right now. It took him to get me here.

I look up and catch his awaiting smile. *God, he's beautiful.*

"You ready?"

I think it takes me a second, but I eventually force myself out of my trance.

"Hmm?"

"To go?" he asks.

"Oh. Yeah," I say, nodding my head.

"I'll just have to get the keys to my dad's truck. I'm not quite sure Ol' Red will make it into town."

I laugh softly, as my eyes suddenly get stuck on something in the corner.

"What about that?"

I point to a motorcycle in the back of the garage and watch Jorgen's eyes follow my gesture to the bike.

"Oh that?" he asks.

I nod my head.

"That's my old Harley. I bought that before I even got my license and fixed it up. It runs pretty well."

He stops and shoots me a sideways smirk.

"Do...you...want to take that?" he asks, timidly.

I think about it for a split second. Then, before I have the chance to change my mind, I nod my head.

"But you're in a dress."

I shrug my shoulders. "Well, technically, it's a skirt, but I'll make do."

I watch his smile carve a wide path across his face.

"All right, let's go," he says.

He disappears into the garage for a second and comes back out with two old, black helmets. My heart jumps at the helmets' color.

"Come on," he says.

I slowly follow him over to the bike. There's a part of me that can't believe what I'm about to do, and then there's another part of me that just can't wait to feel the wind on my bare arms and legs again.

I watch Jorgen swing one leg over the bike and straddle it. Then, he turns and pats a part of the black leather seat behind him. I try to move, but I'm frozen. I just can't seem to pick up my foot and take the first step.

"Come on," he says again, smiling and waving me closer toward him.

I suck in a big breath. My heart is racing now. I can feel its thuds hitting hard against the wall of my chest. I even feel as if I can hear its beats. But Jorgen's eyes are comforting somehow in a weird way. I haven't figured out why yet. Maybe blue is just a comforting color. I try to pick up my foot again, and this time, it moves. And before I know it, I'm swinging my leg over the bike and resting a foot on each peg. I take a second then and let it sink in that I'm on the bike—that I'm on a bike for the first time since... I stop the thought, close my eyes and let the breath I've held hostage in my lungs for the last minute slowly escape my lips.

"Helmet," he says, handing it to me.

I take it and carefully squeeze it over my head before he twists around and takes the straps underneath my chin and snaps them together.

"It fit okay?"

I nod my head. The big helmet nods with me.

"Good," he says. "First time you've ever been on a bike?"

I will my heart not to drop to the bottom of my stomach.

"A Harley...yes," I manage to say.

"Okay, you should probably hold on," he says, smirking back at me.

I wrap my arms around his midsection, somewhere between his waist and his chest. I purposefully lay my hands flat against his body so that I can feel every muscle.

"You ready?"

I think about his question, but clearly, not long enough because the next thing I know, my head is nodding *yes*—even though I'm not so sure if I'll ever truly be ready for this.

"All right," I hear him say. "Nice and tight."

I squeeze him tighter and then hear the puttering start of the engine. A few moments later, I feel the force pushing me backwards and the loose gravel on the driveway giving way under the tires. But then, I also feel the wind hit my arms and legs, and I close my eyes. There's adrenaline, and there's fear, but mostly, I just feel the wind. I feel the parts warmed by the sun and those pockets cooled by the shade. Every breath of summer air brushes over me, dancing and swirling, and ultimately, carving new memories deep into the pores of my skin.

Chapter Twenty

Fair

"There are three things that you have to do at a county fair," Jorgen says, flashing me his now famous crooked smile.

"And what are those three things?" I ask.

He holds out one finger. "Number one. You must get a funnel cake."

"Dessert?" I ask.

"Dessert," he confirms.

We stop at a food-truck-looking thing with an opening on one side and a big whiteboard on the other. On the whiteboard, there's a list of fruits and sweets scribbled down two columns.

"You've had a funnel cake before, right?"

I purse my lips in deep thought. And eventually, I shake my head.

"No?" he asks.

He looks so shocked or offended—I don't know which—that it makes me laugh.

"Isn't it just a bunch of fried dough or something? I've had a doughnut before."

"No, no, no, sweetie," he says, as if adding the term of endearment takes away the horror in his voice. "Doughnuts and funnel cakes are not the same."

He asks the woman in the truck for a plain cake with extra powdered sugar.

"Your first one has to be plain," he explains. "And when you graduate from that, we can start adding the toppings. But if you ask me, I think plain's the best anyway."

I give him my best apprehensive look. He just smiles and eventually takes a paper plate from the woman. Then, he pulls off a piece of the cake and holds it up to my lips.

I hesitate but then open my mouth. And after chewing the piece of cake a few seconds, I look up and meet his awaiting stare.

"It's good," I say. "It's actually really good." I swallow and then shake my head. "It's not really like a doughnut at all."

"See, what did I tell ya?"

I pull off another big piece. "What are the other two things?" I ask, taking a bite.

He clears his throat as if preparing to reveal a well-kept secret.

"Ride at least one ride," he says, proudly. "And pet a sheep."

I stop chewing and fix my eyes on his. "What?"

He only shrugs his shoulders and nods his head.

"Pet a sheep?" I ask.

"Yeah," he says. "It's fun. Oh, and you've got to go to the tractor pull. That's the last thing."

"But wait, that's four things," I say.

He grabs my hips and playfully pulls my side closer to his as we start walking.

"I could have sworn you were a writer, but now I'm starting to believe you actually might be an undercover mathematician." He narrows one eye at me. "I thought I knew you, Ada Cross." His last words are raspy, and surprisingly, really seductive.

I try to shake off his sexy voice with a guarded laugh.

"Okay," he says. "So, what ride do you fancy, my dear?"

I scan the area where all the rides seem to be. I know virtually nothing about rides or fairs, for that matter. I think I went to a county fair when I was little back in Independence, but I don't remember much about it. I'm sizing up the whole place when suddenly, my eyes fall onto a tall contraption, circling high above the grassy field below it. And I know just enough to know what it is.

"The Ferris wheel," I say.

I'm not sure, but I think my eyes light up as if I'm seven or something all over again.

"Good choice," he says.

He picks up the last piece of funnel cake and throws the paper plate into a metal trash can.

"It's all yours," he says, holding it out toward me.

I open my mouth, and he feeds me the last piece.

"Mmm," I say, chewing. "I'm really going to have to learn how to make these."

He just grins at me and takes my hand. The ride hasn't started, so we hurry to it. And when we reach a set of metal gates, Jorgen shows the man taking tickets our wrist bands. The man nods, then lifts a metal bar from the bench, and Jorgen and I both squeeze into the seat and pull the bar to our laps. It doesn't take me long to realize just how perfectly close I am to Jorgen in the little bench, and it makes me sport a cheesy grin. I try to hide it by sitting back, but suddenly, the bench moves. I quickly throw my hands to the bar in front of us and straighten up again.

"Is this safe?" I ask, sounding terrified.

Jorgen laughs. "You've got a habit of askin' that after the fact, don't ya?"

I push out a nervous laugh, but then I quickly go to examining the bench, checking to make sure everything's connected and that all the screws look tight.

"Tell me you've been on a Ferris wheel before."

I stop and look at him.

"I have, but I was little, and I don't remember the seat moving."

"Honey, the swing's the best part about this ride. Otherwise, you're just goin' in one big circle at a turtle's pace."

"I don't mind turtle pace," I admit.

I notice Jorgen's eyes turn down toward the nonexistent space between us. "I've gotta admit, there are worse things in the world," he says.

I meet his stare. I want to laugh, but something about him makes me just swoon instead. Even when he's being cheesy, he's somehow sexy.

Seconds go by, and his eyes don't leave mine. And unbelievably soon, the world seems to stop. I follow his slow gaze to my lips. My heart races. All I can think about is his kiss as my eyelids fall over my eyes. But before I feel his touch, the seat jolts backwards, catching us both off guard. A sound comes from me. I think it's part terrified, part excited. Whatever it is, I feel Jorgen's arm wrap around me in the next moment, and I lean into him and immediately feel his chest rise and then fall into a sigh. Meanwhile, I swallow hard and try to breathe normally again. If the sudden jolt didn't knock the wind right out of me, missing his kiss did.

In a handful of moments, we're at the top of the wheel and both still recovering, I think, when I timidly peer over the side. People look like tiny Wii game characters now, floating and meandering over the grass below us. But I can also see the river and fields and patches of trees that stretch for miles.

"We're so high." My excited words just fall off my tongue.

Jorgen chuckles and then sends me a sexy smile. I can tell he's still thinking about our almost-kiss. I just lower my eyes and laugh too, solidifying the fact that the missed opportunity didn't go unnoticed.

He chuckles some more and then seems to shake it off as he points off into the distance. "See, way over there. There's a house and a shed and then there's a barn next to it."

"Yeah," I say, spotting the buildings.

"That's my parents' house. And there's the shed where we keep Ol' Red."

I follow his hand to another spot below us. I see the shed, and I also notice the train is gone now.

We go around a few more times, and Jorgen points out the grocery store, the ice cream shop, the corner where he made a lemonade stand with a friend when he was eight—the places that make up his childhood. And it makes me happy—to be exactly where I am—with him.

It feels as if only seconds have passed, and our swing is slowing at the bottom of the wheel. There's a quick halt before the man running the ride magically unlocks the bar above our laps and frees us. Jorgen gets out first and then turns around to help me out of the bench.

I happily take his hand and follow him onto the grassy ground again.

"Now where?" I ask.

He squeezes my hand. "This way."

We head to a big tent in the center of the field. And the closer we get to it, the thicker the waves of smells. They're not all bad—some are, but not all of them. Finally, we get underneath the tent, and just like that, I'm on Noah's Ark—as if someone seriously just collected up every animal they could find around here and then stuck them all under this tent. There are chickens and pigs and rabbits and cows and some other strange-looking animals that look as if they could be some combination of the normal ones.

"Here, touch it," Jorgen says, stopping us in front of a short, wooden fence.

I look at him blankly. Then, I watch him reach over the fence and place his hand on the back of an off-white, spongy-looking creature, and I laugh. "Are you sure we can touch them?"

"Yeah," he says, still stroking the animal.

I take a step closer to the fence and then carefully touch the back of the sheep before quickly pulling my hand back and gasping.

Jorgen just stares at me as if he doesn't know whether he should rescue me or commit me.

"It *is* soft," I say, at last.

His face brightens, and he laughs. Meanwhile, I find my hand gravitating toward the sheep's back again, and within no time, my fingers are caressing its thick fur or wool or whatever the soft, spongy stuff is.

"This *is* fun," I exclaim.

He shrugs his shoulders and cocks his head. "I've never found anyone who didn't like pettin' a sheep."

Just then, a loud engine roars from somewhere outside the tent. It makes me jump, but it doesn't seem to faze any of the animals meandering in their little pens around us.

I look at Jorgen with gaping eyes.

"Tractor pull," he simply says.

"Aah." I nod my head and watch him brush his hands together and then lean up against the fence.

"Well, now that you've got your sheep-petting fix, you wanna head on over?" he asks.

My eyes fall onto the animal again that's now busy gnawing on something near the ground.

"One more time," I say, reaching over the fence and gently pressing my fingers into the sheep's soft back.

Jorgen just shakes his head and smiles.

We watch the fourth thing on the to-do list—the tractor pull—until the day is swallowed by the night and then some. And Jorgen tries to teach me all he knows about tractors and tractor pulls. I mostly just watch the way his eyes light up when one charges past us. And I notice after awhile that there's a direct correlation between the level of his excitement and how far down the track one gets before it's suddenly jerked backwards. Then eventually, a tractor races across the dirt in front of us and comes to a halting stop right before everyone stands, claps and starts moving again.

"Is it over?"

"Yeah," he says. "Until next year."

He stands up from the wooden bench, and I follow his lead, while dusting off the back of my skirt.

"Now, we wait for the best part of the night."

I stop dusting and look up at him.

"Jorgen Ryker, I believe that makes five things now that we must do at a county fair."

"Oh, but you don't have to do anything for this one, my dear. All you have to do is watch."

He tugs at my hand, and together, we climb down the wooden bleachers and make our way to a little, grassy hill that overlooks an empty field.

"This looks pretty good," he says, coming to a stop.

He eyes the grass and then sits down. I do the same and sit down right next to him, as people gradually gather around us.

"What are we waiting for?" I whisper, after a little while.

He simply smiles at me. "You'll see."

Just then, a high-pitched scream and a fiery line shoot from the earth to the starry sky. And suddenly, a burst of color explodes against a black backdrop and lights up the patch of grass where we sit. A loud thud follows, and then another scream and another fiery line shoot to the sky.

I find Jorgen's eyes. He takes my hand and laces his fingers in mine as if my hand belongs in his, and then I return my attention to the sky. I'm not sure what I like more: the dancing lights or the way his large, rough hand seems to swallow mine.

One by one, blues and whites and reds and golds shoot to the sky, burst and then fall toward the earth like bits of dust and disappear. It goes on like this until at last there's a thunderous stream of colors soaring to the heavens all at once. It looks as if the field in front of us is bursting into one big firework. I try to make my eyes as wide as I can to soak in all the madness. Then, just like that, it's black again.

I glance up at Jorgen, and I don't even need a mirror to know there's a childish excitement written all over my face. It's stupid and probably goofy-looking, but I don't care. "I like fireworks."

He lowers his head and chuckles to himself. "Good. Me too."

I watch him lean back on the ground and fold his hands behind his head. He makes himself comfortable in the grass, and then, his eyes meet mine. Those baby blues seem to tempt me first right before he reaches for my arm and gently pulls me down next to him.

"You can't leave the fair without lookin' at the stars."

I let him guide me down onto the warm, little spikes of grass as I make a mental note: That's six things to do at the county fair.

He stretches out his arm and pats his bicep. "Pillow."

I shoot him a curious glance.

"I know it's hard, but it's all I've got."

I start to laugh as I gently rest my head onto his arm. And when I'm settled in, he pulls me closer to him and kisses my forehead. And immediately, my laughter fades.

"Did you...," I start and then stop. "Did you just... kiss me?"

There's a moment where I swear there's not a single emotion written on his face. Then gradually, his lips start to turn up.

"No," he whispers.

I cock my head to the side. "I think you did."

"No," he says again, shaking his head.

By now, I'm completely and utterly mesmerized by the sea in his eyes and the all-consuming thought of his lips on mine.

156

"This is a kiss, Miss Cross," he says, cradling the back of my head in his hand and pulling me closer to his lips.

I search his hooded eyes searching mine until his eyelids close and I can't see the sea anymore. I don't move. I just close my eyes and pray for his lips to touch mine. It seems like an eternity waiting, but then I feel him, and I instantly melt. I melt into his soft, tender lips. I melt into the way he tastes, and in this moment, I'm completely his. I move my lips over his, and I feel his hand move across my jaw. He pulls me closer to him, and I let him. I let him control me, and the way he does it is so gentle and strong and sexy and perfect, and yet, I feel a rebellious tear pressing against my eyelid, threatening to escape.

Our lips eventually break, even though I'm not sure I want them to yet. He pulls my body into his and wraps his strong arms around me. I feel his hard muscles press against my soft skin. My heart dances in my chest, and a wide smile scurries to my happy lips, but soon, I'm reminded of the tear in my eye. I'm not sure why it's there. Maybe it's because I'm so happy or maybe it's because I'm a little sad. I push it back, back as far as I can, though, and bury it in the deepest part of my mind. I'm happy tonight.

And suddenly, I sense his lips near my ear, and then, I feel his breaths touch my skin. It gives me goose bumps and sends excited chills down my spine.

"I'm so happy you're here, Ada." His voice is a whisper, and the way he says my name makes it sound as if it's the prettiest name in all the world.

I take a second and let his seductive, soft words soak into my pores.

"I'm happy I'm here too," I whisper in my next breath.

It's quiet then, to where all you can here are some tree frogs singing and a couple crickets chirping in the background.

"You know," he says, softly, breaking the silence, "my mom and dad met here almost thirty years ago."

"Really?" I ask, snuggling closer to him.

"Yeah, my dad said he took one look at my mom and knew he was gonna spend the rest of his life with her."

He stops, and I can hear him smile before he continues. "The story goes she was eatin' a funnel cake with her friends, and my dad marched right up to her and told her he was going to marry her."

He pauses. "This is the part in the story where my mom takes over. She says the only thing my dad left with that night was the powdered sugar from her funnel cake all over his shirt."

He squeezes me closer to him. "My dad, however, will tell you a different story."

I run my finger gently over his chest, making little swirls on his tee shirt. "What does he say?" I ask.

His chest rises slowly and then falls. "He'll tell you he left that night with my mom's heart."

I smile at his words. "Well, what do you think?"

A low, soft chuckle fills the air before he speaks. "Don't ever tell my mom, but I think my dad's got the right story."

My finger stops grazing his chest. "That's really sweet, Jorgen."

"Yeah, well, I told you he was a sentimental old fart."

I laugh softly into his muscles. Something tells me the apple doesn't fall too far from the tree.

I feel Jorgen's arms wrap tighter around my body then, and he holds me for several perfect moments, until he starts to pull away and then stops.

"What's that?"

I follow his stare to the top of my hip, and then I see it, staring back at me. A wave of air tunnels through my lungs and then pushes forcefully past my lips. I can't help but think if it were just a little darker, he might not have ever noticed it.

"Another stupid idea," I mumble.

"You have a tattoo?"

He finds my eyes and just flashes me a curious, mischievous smile. "Just an *A*?" he asks.

I glance at the small tattoo. It is just an *A*—in black ink. No hearts. No frilly flowers. Just the letter *A*.

"I was just a kid," I say.

"For Ada?" he asks.

I shake my head, and he cocks his to the side.

"Ant...eater?" he asks again before I can stop him.

"No," I say, starting to laugh.

"Aardvark?"

I shake my head. "No."

"Antelope?"

I can't stop giggling as I bury my head into his hard chest. "No," I say.

His finger regains my attention when I feel its tip lightly tracing the *A*, and soon, my laughter fades. I love that little *A*, but sometimes I wish it weren't there. I wish it weren't there to remind me—to make me sad. Without warning, I feel a sigh fall from my lips.

"It used to mean something," I say. "But now it just stands for *always*, as in permanent—something I can never wash away."

He follows a trail with his fingertips from the tattoo to my waist to the side of my ribs, then to my shoulders and finally to my lips.

"I like it," he says, simply. "It's part of you."

I try to smile. He's right, but what he doesn't know is that even without the tattoo, the *A* is still part of me.

"It's part of you, and that's why I love it," he whispers.

He stops in my eyes and just stays there for a while, as if he's reading my soul.

"I'm glad I found you, Ada," he says, placing gentle kisses on my lips and forehead, making me feel as if, somehow, I belong here—to this moment, to this new life, to him.

I close my eyes, and I push everything back. I push it all back as I nestle my cheek against his chest and concentrate on his fingertips roaming up and down my arm. He's tracing little circles on my skin, and it's making me feel as if I could just melt into him—as if at any moment, I could just awake from this beautiful dream and not be able to tell anymore where he ends and I begin.

Chapter Twenty-One

The Tattoo

I don't know how long we've been lying in the grass when I feel a cool breeze brush over my skin. I reach down and tug at my tank top, and my finger brushes the part of my hip where I know the *A* eternally rests. I stop, and then I feel Jorgen's arm pulling me closer into him. I let him pull me, and then I rest my head on his chest again. His body is warm. It's a sharp contrast to the cool night air that has settled in. I snuggle up to him and then close my eyes. But on the back of my eyelids is the letter *A*, and before I can stop my mind from wandering, it goes back four long years and stops in a tire swing under a sleepy, old oak...

"Andrew, let's get tattoos."

Andrew stops the tire with both hands, forcing my chest to collide softly against the thick, braided rope from which it dangles.

"That's crazy," he says, staring straight into my eyes.

I feel my smile starting to fade.

"And you know I love crazy," he adds. He flashes me a wild grin, then starts to push the tire again. "When do we go?"

"Today," I say, feeling the life return to my face.

"What do we get?"

I think about it for a second. "What about each other's names?"

"Perfect," he says.

We walk into the tattoo parlor. It's not that scary, but I think the image I had in my mind was aimed to prepare me for the worst-case scenario. Even the peach vinyl, dentist-looking chair in the back doesn't look all that menacing. The place is small, and there are ink designs completely covering the walls, but it's clean. And after I had dreamed up the spur-of-the-moment idea, I had told myself that that's all that really mattered—that it was clean.

I let a breath slowly pass through my lips when I feel Andrew squeeze my hand.

"You can change your mind anytime," he whispers to me.

I shake my head. I'm not changing my mind.

He studies me for an instant, then flashes me a knowing smile and plants a hard kiss on my lips.

Andrew doesn't even flinch as the guy covered from head to toe in tattoos presses Logan *into his chest with a huge electric needle.*

"Does it hurt?" I ask.

Andrew scrunches up his face a little. "It's not that bad."

I've heard that tattoos hurt, but maybe it's all a big ploy to discourage kids from getting them. It seems as though the guy might as well be painting my name into Andrew's chest with the felt tip of a permanent marker. Andrew's face is fearless. In fact, I can't even see an ounce of pain written on it.

I watch the guy covered in tattoos meticulously follow along the letters already outlined on Andrew's chest with his big needle, until he eventually stops and backs away, allowing Andrew and I to examine the new ink.

"It's kind of red," I say.

"It'll be like that for a little while, but it'll go away," the guy with the needle chimes in.

I study the tattoo again and then give the man my seal of approval before he covers it with a big piece of gauze.

"My turn," I say, all but pushing Andrew out of the big, peach chair and climbing into it myself.

I get comfortable and then look up and catch Andrew hovering ominously above me.

"Now, you sure about this, babe?" he asks. "It won't wash off."

I laugh at the seriousness that seems to have devoured his face all of a sudden.

"You mean he's not using washable markers?"

Andrew pretends to scold me with his eyes.

"I'm ready," I say then, turning my attention to the needle guy.

The guy walks away and then comes back a minute later and transfers a stencil onto my skin.

"How does that look?" he asks.

I look at my hip. In small, pretty cursive lettering is Andrew's name.

"Perfect," I say.

The guy nods his head in satisfaction and then puts the needle to the skin on my hip, and it's not so bad. I smile wide up at Andrew, and I almost laugh when he takes my hand. Whoever said getting a tattoo was painful was nothing but a...

My train of thought stops the moment I feel a sharp, gigantic needle digging a deep, rugged trench into my skin. I let out a squeal and squeeze Andrew's hand as if my life depends on it. But the needle keeps tearing a jagged path into my hip. I bite my bottom lip—hard—and silently take everything back about tattoos being painless.

"You tricked me," I shout. "You acted like this didn't hurt."

I try to sound playful, but I'm pretty sure it only comes out pained. Andrew scrunches up his face in pity.

"I'm sorry, babe," he says, sandwiching my hand in between both of his.

I close my eyes, and I feel warm tears welling up behind my eyelids.

"Okay," Andrew suddenly rattles off. "A. A looks good. We're stopping at A."

The needle guy picks up his torture device.

I look up from my agony and stare down at my hip. "But he's not finished."

"Baby, I think the A looks cool by itself. My whole name will be too much."

I look down at my hip again and then up at the guy holding the needle. He clings to my gaze for a second, seemingly waiting for my permission to proceed. But then, I notice him glance at Andrew and then back at me, and then his mouth opens.

"Just the A looks pretty cool too."

The needle guy is frozen in his place. His face tells me that Andrew got to him. I sigh and look one last time at the unfinished tattoo before I find Andrew again. He's smiling; it seems pained, but he is smiling.

I know having Andrew *in the little letters would have looked just fine because it looks just fine in the stencil that's already there. But I'm also kind of happy that Andrew hates watching my pain just as much as I hate going through it.*

"The A *it is," I finally say to the man holding the big needle.*

Jorgen lifts his head, and the old memory vanishes just as quickly as it had appeared.

"You ready to go?" He whispers low and near my ear.

I tighten my arm around his chest. "Do we have to?"

He pauses for a moment.

"No," he says and then lays his head back down. I feel his hand brush down my body and stop at the small of my back. "I could stay like this forever."

Chapter Twenty-Two

Home

"Are you singing?"

Oh, God, he heard me. How could he have heard me?

"No..." I scrunch up my face and cringe a little—hoping maybe he'll believe me, even though I know he won't. I already hear him smiling over there.

"You were." He looks over at me, flashes me a big, toothy grin and then sets his eyes back on the road.

I try to hide my smile as my own gaze gets stuck too on the solid, white line guiding our way.

The interstate is quiet. It's dark outside the truck. It's dark inside too, except for the little blue light coming from the dash. I watch as Jorgen glances over at me again, then switches his hands on the wheel and reaches for my hand. I let him take it and cradle it in his as another song comes on the radio and I turn my attention back to the dark highway. My heart skips a little in my chest. I press my lips together and try not to make it obvious that I'm smiling to myself. I just can't seem to get over the way my hand feels in his.

A moment goes by, maybe, before I hear Jorgen mumble something, and it forces my eyes back to the driver's seat. Then, all of a sudden, a string of lyrics rolls off his tongue: "You and me goin' fishin' in the dark..."

He says the lyrics more than he sings them, taking every chance he gets to look over at me.

"Lyin' on our backs and countin' the stars," he sings, growing louder as the song goes on.

It's cute the way he tries to make the words sound like the original singer. He's no rock star, but then, neither am I. I just look at him and smile. The song is by Nitty Gritty Dirt Band. I don't know most country songs, but my grandpa used to listen to this one, so I know this one.

"Where the gre-en grass gro-ws," he continues, dragging out each word.

My eyes dart to his, and I start to laugh. "Those aren't the words."

He just flashes me a crooked grin and keeps going, but now, I can't help but join in. At least I know all the words.

"Stayin' the whole night through," we sing together. "Feels so good...to beeee...withhhh...you..."

We sing the rest of the song. He adds his own words at random, and eventually, I do too. And then we laugh until the next one comes pouring through the speakers. It's a ballad and not nearly as easy to sing to. The cab grows quiet again—but only for a few seconds.

167

"This was so much fun," I say, turning so that I can get a good look at him and his dark, wavy hair. He's got a strong, five-o'clock shadow now, and only one hand is on the wheel. And there's a blue tint to him because of the lights from the dash, but it only seems to add to his smoldering look.

"Pretending we know how to sing?" He chuckles.

"No, well, yeah, that too," I say. "But I mean this whole weekend. I had my first funnel cake and went to my first tractor pull, and believe it or not, petted my first sheep."

He glances over at me and gives me a sexy wink. "You never knew this country boy was so cultured, did ya?"

I squeeze his hand and smile.

"What was your favorite?" he asks.

I think about it for a second. Then, I close my eyes and contemplate it a little bit longer.

"Ol' Red," I finally say.

He laughs once, and I watch his eyes venture away from the road and onto me. "Why that old thing?"

"I don't know. Because I like the way you look in it."

"What?" He sounds surprised.

"I like the way you look in it," I repeat, with more conviction this time. "You look like you belong, you know?"

"Like I belong in an old truck?"

His scrunched-up face makes me laugh.

"Yeah...no. Well, sort of," I stumble. "You looked comfortable, like you didn't have a care in the world—like you were home."

He takes his eyes off the road and just smiles at me.

"What?" I ask. "That sounds crazy, doesn't it?"

His face shifts back to the highway, but then I notice his head slowly shaking back and forth.

"It wasn't the truck, Ada."

I furrow my eyebrows. "Hmm?"

"It wasn't the truck that made me feel like I was home," he says again. "It wasn't even being home that made me feel like I was home."

Little wrinkles form at the corners of his eyes as his slow gaze ventures away from the highway and lands on me. And just like that, his eyes are soft again.

"It was you, Ada. Being next to you in Ol' Red made me feel like I was finally home."

I take a second and let the moment sink in, and before long, it almost feels as if my heart is shattering into a thousand tiny pieces and just falling to the floorboards at my feet. His words are so raw, so honest. They remind me of a way I used to feel. And without another thought, I unsnap my seatbelt, then slide into the little seat next to him and snap the lap belt over my legs. And suddenly, it's as if I'm seventeen all over again.

He lifts his arm and wraps it around my shoulders. Then, he pulls me closer, and I rest my head against him and listen to the new song that's now softly pouring through the speakers.

I don't tell him—only because I think he already knows—but he's beginning to feel like home to me too.

Chapter Twenty-Three

The Dream

"**Y**ou're so cute when you sleep."

I turn my head over on my pillow.

"Andrew," I whisper.

He's standing in the doorway. His honey-blond hair with its sprinkled russet streaks sweeps across his forehead and covers the tops of his ears.

"Let's run away together," he says, taking the few steps from the door to my bed.

Instantly, I feel a happy grin shoot across my face.

"Okay," I whisper.

He lies down beside me, puts his arm around my waist and pulls me closer to him. I let him do it, but as he does, I stare into his dark brown eyes. I just keep searching them, trying to make sure they're real, until suddenly, I feel tears start to fill my own eyes.

"Baby, don't cry," I hear him say, bringing the back of his finger to a place under my eye and wiping away my tears.

I try to laugh because his eyes are real, and he's really here with me, and I have nothing to cry about.

"We were a small-town scandal, weren't we?" I ask, through my tears.

He keeps his eyes in mine for several moments. He's wearing a smile, but it's faint.

"What if we never would have...," I begin.

"Shh," he says softly, as he breaks his stare from my eyes and moves his lips to my ear.

"Logan, we weren't a scandal," he whispers. "We were in love."

I take a minute and let his last word echo through my ear, and then through my mind and finally, through my soul. Then, I grab a hold of it and tuck it away inside my heart.

"Andrew," I say and then stop and wait for his eyes to find mine again.

"What, babe?"

"Is there hope for us?"

He pauses and draws a long breath.

"For us...I don't know, baby," he says, at last, forcing the air out of his lungs. "But for you, yes."

I watch his lips gradually turn up at one end.

"Hope is a funny thing when you think about it," he goes on. "It's always right in front of you."

My gaze falters and falls to the pillow.

"You just have to see it," he whispers.

I look back up into his eyes and then sigh.

"Andrew."

"What, babe?"

"I miss you," I say.

He squeezes me tighter, and I can smell his cologne on his tee shirt. I breathe it in until I feel as if my lungs are going to explode.

"Andrew," I say again.

"Yes, baby?"

"Let's go to Paris," I say. "I always wanted to go to Paris with you. Will you go with me?"

I watch his lips quiver, trying to turn up, but they don't ever make it to a smile. And instantly, I feel the warm tears pressing against my eyelids again because I know what that look means.

"Okay," he says, slowly nodding his head. "We'll go to Paris."

He takes my hand.

"We'll go tomorrow," he whispers.

"No," I say.

I start to shake my head.

"No," I cry.

There are tears falling down my cheeks like rain now.

"We have to go today," I cry. "Life will tear us apart, Andrew. We don't have tomorrow."

Suddenly, my eyes open, and I'm frozen. I look around the room. Everything is normal and still and quiet. I wonder why I'm awake, and then it hits me. I quickly turn over and look to my left. There's no one there. I lose my next breath, and my heart sinks. I reach up and touch my cheeks. There are no tears on them, but I feel as if there should be.

I take a deep breath in and then slowly push it right back out again before I peel the covers back and sit up on the side of the bed. I really hate my dreams sometimes.

And I can't even call them nightmares because I love them too. I love them, but I hate them because I can't stay in them. They're my tortured dreams.

I close my eyes and try to replay every moment of the dream in my head. I try to replay his boyish, raspy words and his warm, soft breaths against my skin. I try to remember the smell of his cologne and the perfect way his shaggy hair fell across his ears. I try to replay it all— exactly the way it used to be. And then I get to the part where I realize exactly the way it is, and my heart aches.

"No," I cry.

I double over and cradle my face in my hands. I miss him. I miss his voice; I miss the certain, special ring it used to have to it that always made me feel loved. I try to recall the hum of his words, the ebb and flow of every syllable as it trailed off his lips. In my dream, the voice sounded perfect—like a song, my favorite song—but now, I can't hear it anymore.

I want to go back and change everything. I can't help but think that if we never would have gotten married that day, that things might have been different. It might all have played out differently if we had just waited. And maybe it was karma—getting back at us for eloping or for being too young.

I pull open my nightstand drawer. In a corner, under the marriage license and a birthday card from Hannah, I slide out a ring and slip it on. At least Hannah hadn't found this. I twist the ring slowly around the base of my finger with my thumb. And I let my eyes get lost in its little diamond and its little, breakable promise inside. Then, after a moment, I fold my other hand over the ring and bring both hands to my chest.

"Forever and a day," I whisper to myself, before I slowly slide the ring off and carefully tuck it away again, underneath the marriage license and the birthday card. And then I close the drawer.

Chapter Twenty-Four

Come Over

I glance at the clock on my nightstand. It's 5:30 and still dark outside. The sun hasn't even come up yet, but I'm wide awake—thanks to my dream and evidentially, the chains of my past. I rub my eyes and reach for my phone. The light from its screen blinds me—as if I were looking straight into the sun. I snap both eyes shut and wait a second. And when I finally get the courage to peek through one eye again, I notice there's a message waiting on the screen. It was sent at 2 o'clock in the morning. I click on it and read:

Can't sleep. Thinking about you. Had the best weekend! Can't wait to see you today!

I stare at the words for another minute before I set the phone back down. I feel torn—torn between my old life and my new one, between letting go and moving on. Images of my dream are still playing in my head—images of Andrew and the way his lips moved when my name—my birth name—came tumbling off of them—and Paris. I force my eyes shut, swallow hard and lie back down. I lie there until the images in my mind start to fade and eventually disappear.

People say it all gets better in time. And I think it does. Each day is a little better than the last; each dream pulls me back just a little bit less. But what they don't say is how much time it takes. They don't tell you how many more moments your heart will race, sink, tear or ache. They don't tell you how many more breaths you'll lose over a memory, a dream, a scent, a spoken name. They don't tell you how long it will take to heal. They don't even tell you what being "healed" actually feels like because I'm pretty sure I'll never feel like I did when I was sixteen—years before my world crashed in on me. But what they do tell you is that it does get better and that *time* is part of that equation. So, I guess for now, I'll just wait on *time*.

I lie there for another minute, until I feel as if I just can't lie there anymore, and I pick up the phone and read over the message from Jorgen again. And this time, a smile instinctively dances to my lips.

I type in a few letters asking him if he's up yet and hit *send*. Then I wait. And within a couple seconds, there's a response: *Yes. You?*

My fingers go to typing another sentence before hitting *send* again.

Seconds later, the phone beeps and lights up, and I look down at the screen: *Get your cute butt over here then!*

176

I laugh to myself, then stand up and make my way to the door. On the way out, I tame my hair into a ponytail and grab a piece of gum sitting on the counter and shove it into my mouth.

Three steps later, I'm at Jorgen's door. I knock softly a couple times and wait, but no one answers.

"Jorgen," I softly say.

I wait a few more seconds. Then, I slowly turn the knob, and the door cracks open.

I hesitate but then step inside. The little rooms are dark, and there's still no sign of him. So, either he sleeps with his door unlocked, which is completely crazy, or he's already unlocked it and gone back to bed. How long was I messing with my hair?

"Jorgen," I say, barely over a whisper, as I make my way to the back of the apartment. Now, I think I'm expecting him, at any moment, to jump out at me from some dark corner.

There's no answer.

"Jorgen," I whisper again.

I wait. Nothing.

I finally get to his bedroom and freeze in the doorway when I see him.

He's there—in his bed. He looks perfect. His eyelids are covering his eyes, and his thick eyelashes are resting on his cheekbones. His short, barely-there curls are tossed every which way on his pillow. The covers are strewn all about him; one leg is sticking out. I lean up against the door frame and just watch him sleep for a few moments. I love him. I'm scared to say it out loud. I'm scared to even think it, but I do. I have fallen for the paramedic across the hall—the normal, motorcycle-driving, blue-eyed, abs of steel paramedic that lives exactly three steps from my door.

177

He turns over, and it snaps me out of my trance. I watch him tuck the comforter under his chin and stop moving again. Then, I tiptoe over to the side of the bed closest to me and lie down beside him. He doesn't even flinch. I lay my head on the pillow next to his head and blow a gentle stream of warm air onto one set of his eyelashes. It doesn't faze him. I wait a second and then blow a gentle breeze onto the other set. His head rolls the other way but then returns to mine a second later. I'm trying not to laugh as I blow another stream of warm air onto his lips. He twitches and then suddenly, his eyelashes flutter open.

"Hey," he says in a deep, sleepy voice. "What took you so long?"

I plant a light kiss on his unshaven cheek.

"I had to wait for you to finish dreaming evidently."

He squints his eyes and wrinkles his brow.

"Come here," he says, grabbing my hips and pulling me closer to him. "I had a dream about you."

"You did?" My cheek presses up against his bare chest.

"Yeah, I dreamt you wore something other than that sweatshirt and those boxers to bed."

I lift my head.

"That was your whole dream?"

"Well, no, but the rest is R-rated."

I laugh and rest my head on his chest again. "Jorgen Ryker," I scold playfully.

He's quiet for a second before I hear his raspy voice again.

"My mom ordered your magazine."

"Yeah?" I ask.

"Yeah. She loved you. My whole family loved you."

"Really?" I scrunch up my face and timidly peer up at him.

"Really," he confirms.

A little wave of excitement overtakes me. I wanted them to like me. And if I were being honest, I wanted them not only to like me but also to think of me as a good match for their son too.

"I really liked them too," I say.

We're both quiet again for a moment.

"Ada."

"Hmm?" I ask.

"You're my summer night."

I feel my face molding into a question mark. For a second, I wonder if he's still dreaming.

"I am?" I ask, peeking up at his sleepy face. His eyes are closed, but there's a faint smile hanging on his lips.

"Yeah." He nods. "And my blue-sky afternoon and my rainy Sunday...and...my open road."

I push out a laugh.

"All those things?" I ask.

"Every one," he confirms.

"Well..." I lace my fingers in his. "You're my..." I think about it and let a few silent moments pass. "My sea otter."

"What?" he asks.

"My sea otter," I say again, with more confidence.

"Are you trying to tell me something?"

"Well," I say, playing with his thick hair, "if you puffed up your hair a little, and if you grew out your whiskers a little more..."

"Oh really?"

He laughs, and I do too.

"No, I mean you're my figurative sea otter."

"Your figurative sea otter?" He narrows a playful eye at me.

"Yeah," I say, "when they sleep on the water, one holds the other's hand so she doesn't drift away from him."

I feel his hand squeeze mine a little tighter.

"I won't let you drift away," he whispers near my ear.

I can tell he rests his head back on the pillow, and then he's quiet again. His last words mean more to me than I think he knows because drifting, for me, is dangerous. It only leads me back—to memories and a broken heart.

"Whose shirt is it anyway?"

My thoughts break instantly, and my eyes fall to my sweatshirt as I let a few seconds pass.

"It's mine," I say.

He laughs. "No, I mean before it was yours."

I don't say anything for a moment. I just swallow—hard.

"It was my high school sweetheart's," I say, at last.

I don't look at him, and he doesn't say anything more about the shirt.

"The boxers?" he asks, sheepishly. "Should I assume the same person?"

I take a second before slowly nodding into his chest.

"Why do you wear them?" he asks.

I angle my face up toward his. "I thought you liked this outfit."

His head lifts slightly. "I said you look good in it. I never said I liked it," he clarifies.

"Aah," I say, sending him a playful smirk. But his eyes only widen, as if he's still waiting for my answer.

"Why do I wear them?" I ask myself, my voice fading off.

My eyes fall to a spot on his tan chest and get stuck there for nearly a minute before I look back up at him and shrug my shoulders. I could tell him why. I could tell him everything right now, but I just can't seem to find the first word.

"You don't still...," he starts but doesn't finish.

I know what he wants to ask: *You don't still love him?*

I shake my head. It's not the true answer to his question, but it is the right one. It's the one that matters.

"Do you want some new pajamas, Ada Bear?"

Ada Bear? I feel a slight smile edging up my face again. I go by a lot of names, but *Ada Bear* has never been one of them. I catch his eyes, and then suddenly, I feel my head slowly nodding. I don't know if it's the new nickname or the way his blues hypnotize me, but I nod without any real thought.

And as if the earth all of a sudden shifts, Jorgen jumps up, grabs a pair of basketball shorts lying on the floor and pulls them over his boxers, then runs to his closet. I sit up on his bed and dangle my feet over the side. I listen to him root around the little room for a while until he finally emerges a minute later. He's holding out a gray sweatshirt with his high school football team's name stretched across its front and a pair of blue, checkered boxers.

I take the shirt and boxers and stare at them clutched within my fingers and lying against the backdrop of the gray and red, checkered cotton of my old life. And when I look back up, Jorgen is smiling a wide, goofy grin, and I can't help but smile too.

"Thank you," I manage to say. "These are perfect."

If it's possible, he looks even more content.

"You want some breakfast?" he asks.

I take in a breath and then nod my head.

"Comin' right up," he says.

I watch him hurry off into the kitchen, and then I hear some clanging of pots and pans before my eyes travel down again to the sweatshirt and boxers in my hands. Then, slowly, I feel my stare moving to the old sweatshirt I'm wearing. I pull its collar up over my nose and breathe in. It doesn't smell like Andrew anymore. It used to smell like his sweat and his cologne. It did for a long time, until one day, it just didn't. And after several days of not being able to smell him, I finally laid the shirt down inside the wash machine, closed the lid and pulled the knob. But as soon as I heard the water pouring into the machine, I flung open the lid and tried to retrieve it. But it was too late. I cried for almost an hour that day, hovered over that soggy sweatshirt. And I still pull it up over my nose every once in a while, just to see if I can smell him again. They say the strongest sense connected to memory is smell. And I believe it because sometimes, if I closed my eyes and breathed him in, I could almost feel him next to me.

I swallow hard, forcing the lump in my throat back down, before standing up and sliding Andrew's boxers off and then sliding on Jorgen's. I fold the red boxers and carefully set them onto the bed. Then, I pull off Andrew's old baseball sweatshirt and force Jorgen's old football shirt over my head. After Jorgen's shirt is on, I carefully fold Andrew's and set it on top of the boxers.

I stare at the folded pile then. Andrew's hooded sweatshirt no longer has a drawstring for its hood. And the cuffs at the ends of each sleeve are tattered and torn. The word *baseball* across the front of the shirt is now just a faded and broken semblance of the word, and there's a tear at the end of one leg on the boxer shorts where I caught it on the arm of my Adirondack chair one day.

The pile looks sad and discarded, and all of a sudden, there's a ripping at my heart, and I want to throw Andrew's sweatshirt and boxers back on as quickly as I can. But instead, my eyes fall to the clothes I'm wearing and get stuck on the blue in my new boxers. I love the color. It reminds me of Jorgen's blue eyes. I tug on the sweatshirt that now all but hangs off my shoulders. It's larger than Andrew's, and it almost feels as if it's swallowing me. I kind of like the way it feels.

"Ada, do you want your eggs scrambled?"

My eyes travel to the kitchen and then eventually fall back onto the little pile of clothes sitting on the bed.

"Yes, please," I call out to him.

I stare at the pile for another minute before scooping it up and making my way into the kitchen. But I only get two steps outside the bedroom door when Jorgen's hungry gaze makes me freeze. His sexy eyes narrow in on mine, and within an instant, he drops the skillet and starts a slow saunter toward me—looking as if he has a million thoughts running through his mind but only one clear goal.

When he gets close enough to touch me, he wraps his strong arms around my body and lifts me off the floor.

"Now, that outfit I love." He trails a soft, deep whisper into my ear.

A shiver runs down my spine, and I almost gasp when he presses his lips to mine and gives me a long, hard, slow kiss. I take it all in—as much as I can—until our lips part, and he gently sets me down again. A strand of my hair has come to rest over my left eye; he takes it and tucks it behind my ear before flashing me a crooked grin and leaving me for the kitchen again.

I have to catch my breath. Sometimes, without warning, he just takes the air right out of me. He's always surprising me somehow—there's always a new, softer or funnier or sexier side of him—as if each day, I'm discovering him all over again. I've really never met anyone like him. He really is an interesting—and beautiful—creature.

I take a moment just to stare at him. A white, sleeveless undershirt stretches across his broad chest now, making his tan biceps look huge. And with his dark, messy hair and scruffy five-o'clock shadow darkening his jaw, he looks as if he just stepped out of an ad for men's cologne or something. Sometimes I wonder if he's even real.

I eventually peel my eyes away from him just long enough to situate the sweatshirt and boxers I had been holding on one stool, and I take a seat on the other.

I don't say anything. I just go back to watching him as he puts two pieces of bread into the toaster and then moves to the stove, adjusts the flame and then turns the bacon over in the skillet with a pair of tongs. He's done this before. Every movement is like clockwork.

"Do you need any help there, Ace?"

I'd rather just watch him and his sexy self, but I also feel a little guilty not helping.

He glances back at me. "Nah, I've got it all under control. You just sit back and relax, baby."

I smile and then prop my elbows up onto the counter and rest my chin in my hands.

"Where'd you learn to do all this?"

He keeps doing what he's doing, but he does find a moment in between flipping and placing some scrambled eggs onto a plate to look back at me.

"This?" he asks, eyeing the stove.

I nod my head.

"My grandma," he says. "She's one hell of a cook."

"What about your mom?"

He laughs. "She's one hell of a woman, but she's no cook."

I laugh to myself as he sets a plate and a tall glass in front of me.

"Scrambled eggs, bacon, toast and orange juice," he says, smiling proudly.

I look down at the plate and breathe in the aroma of breakfast. It's a foreign smell. Breakfast for me is usually just a strawberry cereal bar from a generic, cardboard box.

"Jorgen, this smells and looks so good."

He turns back to the stove, and after another minute, sets another plate and another glass of orange juice onto the counter next to mine. Then, he picks up my old sweatshirt and boxers from the stool and places them on the couch behind us. He's careful with the clothes—almost as if he knows what they mean—meant—to me. The simple gesture makes me feel better somehow.

I wait for him to take a seat in the barstool next to me before I dig into the bacon.

"Mmm," I say, chewing. "I think I'll keep you."

I swallow, and Jorgen finds my big, cheesy grin. I take another bite of the bacon and flash him a quick wink. And just like that, he seems to freeze. I start chewing slower and slower and then finally force myself to swallow. His eyes are serious now.

"I love you, Ada."

I lower my head and feel my heart start to race. I don't even think. I just say what I want to say in this very moment.

"I love you too," I say, lifting my eyes to his.

A grin slowly crawls across his rugged morning face, and then, I watch as he picks up a piece of bacon and takes a big bite.

"You know, this really isn't so bad," he mumbles to himself as he eyes the bacon.

I'm still staring at him when his wide-eyed gaze finally falls onto mine again.

"What?" he asks. "I've loved you since the moment you showed up at my door naked."

Without warning, a soft laugh escapes me. I swear I don't know what I'm getting myself into. I go back to my plate and stick my fork into some scrambled eggs, but I keep an eye on him. And all the while, I can't stop smiling. The three little words I thought I would never be happy to hear again from a man just melted my heart. And he had said them over eggs and bacon, as if it were just another day—as if I should have known all along how he felt about me—as if I should have known all along that he loved me. And I had said them too, and I hadn't shattered; I didn't break. I'm still fully intact. I mean, I had every reason to, but I never gave up on love, not even after... I stop and push the memories back.

I still believe in love. And now, in one morning, I had woken up with my first love, crawled into bed with my new love, shed a layer of my old life, had grown a new one and had said *I love you*—all before finishing my eggs, bacon and toast.

Chapter Twenty-Five

Love

"**W**ell, what do you want to do today, Ada Bear?"

Jorgen picks up my plate and sets it into the sink, while I take in a deep breath and breathe out a smile.

"Nothing. Absolutely nothing."

He nods his head. "Absolutely nothing sounds pretty good to me."

He comes up behind me and kisses me softly on my neck, sending goose bumps down my arms and legs. Then, all of a sudden, he scoops me into his arms.

I laugh out loud and tighten my arms around his neck. He carries me to the couch and lays me gently down, then lies next to me and rests his forehead on mine.

"I do love you," he says.

I let go of a wide grin. "So I've heard."

"You know, I pictured it being more romantic when I said it—like maybe there were fireworks in the background or rose petals on the floor or there was this plane writing it in big cloud letters in the sky. But you just looked so darn cute in my sweatshirt, and you said you liked my bacon; I just had to say it."

I laugh. "I did like your bacon. And I liked that you said it over breakfast."

He's quiet for a moment, but he keeps his eyes in mine. I wish sometimes I could tell what he was thinking.

"I don't know what it is about you, Ada, but I want to be around you all the time. I mean, I know it's only been a few months, but I just know, you know?"

My eyes drop from his. I can feel the heat rushing to my face.

"You're just so dang beautiful," he goes on, brushing a strand of my hair out of my face with the back of his hand, "with your green eyes and your pretty lips and your little nose." He presses his lips to my nose, then pulls away. "But it's not just that. Ada, you make me laugh. And you're grounded. And you really see people, you know?"

My eyes venture back to his. I'm still blushing, but now my eyebrows are also knitting together a little. I'm not sure what he means.

"In your stories—every day—you see more in people," he explains. "You see more than just an old man owning a bunch of old tractors or an eccentric woman who might or might not harbor strange illusions about cats. You can appreciate that some things are strange and you can laugh about them, but you can see past it all too. You see a soul, a life, a heart that beats."

He lowers his eyes. "That sounds really corny."

"No," I say. "It doesn't."

Now, he's blushing. It looks cute on him.

"Well," I say, "if you had my job, you'd learn to do that too."

I watch him slowly shake his head.

"You didn't learn that, Ada. People don't learn that sort of thing. That's a heart thing. You either got it or you don't. That's what my dad always said, anyway."

My gaze gets stuck on the leather in the couch.

"Well," I say, "I might be able to see well enough to tell someone's story, but you actually put your hands to people. I admire that."

I find his blue eyes.

"I really admire what you do—more than you know," I continue. "I can't imagine how much courage it takes to see what you see every day and to still put a smile on your face at the end of it and to still want to get up the next day and do it all over again."

I stop and look away. I don't want him to see my emotions betraying me.

"Thank you," I say.

"Why are you thanking me?"

The words are on my tongue. I want to tell him that someone like him once rescued me, but I let the moment pass instead. I'm afraid I'll fall into a billion, tiny pieces, and I won't be able to put myself back together again.

"Because you probably don't hear it enough," I say instead.

I lock onto his eyes again and fall deep into their shade of blue. Then, all of a sudden, I feel his strong arms tighten around me.

"I had a crush on you even before I saw you naked outside my apartment that first day, Ada Cross," he whispers into my ear.

He loosens his grip on me, and I pull away a little.

"Before?" I question.

"Yeah," he admits, nodding his head. "From afar—from the other side of a magazine article."

He stops and laughs to himself.

"No you didn't," I say, shaking my head.

"Oh, but I did," he confesses. "I fell in love with a writer who saw the good in strange people."

His sexy, crooked grin makes me smile.

"Jorgen." My voice is almost a whisper. "I love you."

He meets my longing gaze and then leans in and kisses my lips. I wish he knew how much those words mean to me and how hard it is for me to say them—not because I don't love him but because I love someone else too—someone who I know will never say the words back to me.

"I love you too, Ada Bear," I hear him whisper into my ear as he pulls me into his arms again. "I love you too, my Ada Bear."

Chapter Twenty-Six

Marriage

"**Y**ou ever think about marriage?"

I almost drop the glass pitcher to the floor when his words hit my ears.

"Uh, what do you mean?" I try my best to quietly clear my throat.

"Like what it'll be like," Jorgen says. "I think about it sometimes."

His eyes wander over to me. His face is scrunched up in thought. "Is that weird?"

I rest the pitcher safely onto the counter.

"No," I say, simply.

I watch him smile softly, seemingly vindicated.

"I think it would be the coolest thing, you know?" he goes on. "Coming home to someone every night and taking trips together and getting to say, 'my wife.'"

My breath hitches as I open the refrigerator door and slide the pitcher onto the top shelf. And when I turn around, I catch him in the living room flipping through my coffee table book full of awkward family photos and smiling to himself.

"Jorgen."

His eyes find mine. I inhale deeply and then slowly force it out. "I have to tell you something."

He hesitates, then sets the book down into his lap. "What is it?"

He's wearing a smile, and it looks as if he's not the least bit prepared for what I'm about to say. It makes me nervous for him—and for me.

"I...," I start and then stop.

I look down and grip the edge of the counter with both hands. I would swear that time had stopped if I couldn't hear the clock on the wall noisily ticking out the seconds. I feel as if someone else has taken control of me. It's as if someone else is about to say what I can't. I squeeze the countertop and open my mouth just as my apartment door bursts open.

"Lada, I have coffee!"

Hannah's cheerful song echoes through my little apartment, cutting straight through the silence, as she takes a step inside and stops when she notices Jorgen.

"Oh hey, Jorgen."

She doesn't seem as thrown off as she had been the first time she had barged into my apartment and had found Jorgen in my living room.

"I didn't know you were off today," Hannah continues. "Here, you can have my coffee."

She tries to hand him her cup.

"No," Jorgen says, smiling and gesturing for her to keep her coffee.

"I only took one sip," Hannah tries to persuade him.

Jorgen smiles wider. "No, it's really okay. I'm not a big coffee drinker anyway."

Hannah flashes him a playful expression of disapproval. "Gotta watch those non-coffee drinkers," she says, turning her attention to me. "They make me nervous—always awake and happy without reason."

Hannah quickly turns back toward Jorgen and smiles. Jorgen returns her smile with his own. Then, Hannah takes a seat on one of the barstools facing me.

"I really should start knocking," she whispers to me.

I nod. "Not a bad idea."

She pushes her lips to one side and then dips her head in agreement. "Noted," she whispers.

Hannah could have picked a better time to come barging in with coffee, but I'm glad she didn't. I want so badly to tell Jorgen everything, but I also think that I just as badly don't want to tell him anything. I wonder sometimes if I could just get by with never saying the words—ever. I wonder if it would even matter if he never knew. But then, I know that's not really possible...or fair. He should know...soon, and I should be the one to tell him.

"So," Hannah says. "We're having a barbeque tomorrow evening."

"We?" I ask.

"Yeah, Mom and I cooked it up. Just the family— and Jorgen, of course."

Hannah sends me a quick, reassuring look that says: *It'll be okay.* And then she dramatically spins around on the stool and faces Jorgen.

"Jorgen, you can come, right?" she asks.

Jorgen looks at me. I try to hide the utter fear I feel inside about a night with Jorgen surrounded by my family. I know Hannah probably doesn't think it's a big deal, but I have never brought anyone home before—not like this. And it is my family we're talking about. I mean, if they didn't feel the need to express their every opinion about certain aspects of my life at every turn, it wouldn't be so bad, and I wouldn't be so terrified—but that also wouldn't be my family.

I force my lips into a faint smile that Jorgen seems to notice.

"I'd love to," he says.

"Great," Hannah exclaims before she glances at her watch and jumps up. "Well, I've got to get going. Just wanted to drop off the coffee and tell you about the barbeque. Lada, call me later. We can figure out a time for tomorrow."

Hannah slips out the door then just as quickly as she had slipped in a few minutes ago, and instantly, my eyes fall on Jorgen. He looks happy and maybe a little nervous. I make my way to the living room and sit down next to him on the couch.

"They'll love you," I say and mean it.

I watch his sky-blue eyes slowly light up. "Well, I'm excited to meet them." His happy gaze lowers and then quickly lifts again, grabbing my attention. "Is there something you wanted to tell me?"

I feel my face going blank until I remember there was something—something I don't want to say anymore and risk losing that beautiful smile hanging on his lips.

"Uh, no," I say, shaking my head.

He takes a wayward strand of my hair and secures it behind my ear.

"I love you, Ada."

I lower my eyes and press my lips together.

"I love you too," I say, eventually leveling my gaze with his again.

Chapter Twenty-Seven

The Tree

"What's this?"

I turn and then sigh once I see what Jorgen's eyes are planted on. We made it through the whole meeting-the-family thing with not so much as a mention of my life before I was nineteen. Even Hannah kept her mouth shut, which is basically a small miracle. But now, it's me who leads him straight into an old memory.

"Is the *L* for Logan?" he asks, eventually.

I slowly nod my head and push my lips to one side.

He glances at me and then turns his attention back to the big oak tree with the heart carved into its bark.

"The *A*—your tattoo?" he asks.

I nod my head again.

He keeps his eyes planted on the tree, but I know he can see me nodding my head. Meanwhile, I spot a rock on the ground near my feet, and I kick it gently around with my shoe.

"Did you ever have a high school sweetheart?" I ask.

A silent moment passes.

"No," he says at last, shaking his head.

I feel my eyes grow wide. "I don't believe you."

"No, really," he says. "I never really paid attention too much to girls in high school. My head was so deep into football—that, and I had eight girls in my class and two of them, that I knew of, were my cousins. And I wasn't really sure about the rest of them either. I was pretty convinced that we were all related somehow or another."

"Wait. But you dated a girl in high school—who wasn't in your class, right?"

His forehead wrinkles, and he seems to think about it for a moment.

"In high school? No, not really," he says. "It was all kind of the same thing. They were all just siblings or cousins of the girls in my class."

I slowly push my lips into a pout. "That's kind of sad."

"What? Why?" he asks.

He's smiling, but he looks completely puzzled.

"Because," I say, "that means you never got to write notes back and forth during fourth hour, and you never got to wear someone's name on the back of your tee shirt during a game or you never broke curfew because you fell asleep in some old hammock somewhere."

He laughs to himself, and it snaps me out of my starry trance.

"What?" I ask.

"There were other ways to break curfew, Ada Bear."

I look at him suspiciously.

"And they didn't involve a hammock," he adds.

"Well, what did they involve?" I'm curious now.

"I don't know, usually a couple trucks, some four wheelers and a sandy river bottom."

"Aah," I say, starting to laugh.

But after a moment, Jorgen grows quiet, and then I notice him shaking his head. "But, yeah, I didn't need a first love."

My eyes instinctively narrow as I wait for him to continue.

But he doesn't continue—not right away. He takes my hands in his, and his blue eyes seem to leave a thoughtful trail from my lips up to my eyes. And the way he looks at me as if he's searching my soul forces my expression to soften.

"I've got my true love right here," he says. "That's all I need."

He pulls me into him, and suddenly, I feel his warm breaths near my ear. "It's all I ever needed," he whispers.

I let myself fall into the muscles in his chest, and I breathe in the scent of his now familiar cologne, and I close my eyes until I feel as if I could just disappear inside his arms.

"And besides," he whispers as he plants a soft kiss on my neck. "We've still got a lifetime of firsts in front of us."

Chapter Twenty-Eight

Amsel

"**J**eez, Ada, you really do smell like a garbage can," Amsel says, following me into my apartment.

He fans the air and laughs as he does it.

"A ferret," I correct him. "I smell like a ferret."

"And they smell like that when they're alive?" he asks.

I give him a sideways look. "Yes," I confirm.

"And someone raises those things?"

"Believe it or not," I say, throwing my computer bag onto a chair and making my way into my bedroom.

"Ada, honey, you've gotta get a new hobby," he calls out after me.

I come out of my room a few seconds later with a bathrobe wrapped around me.

"But it's the only hobby I have that pays, Amsel," I say, sending him a wink.

He looks my way and laughs. "Well, do us both a favor and wash the stink off of ya all ready."

I shoot him a sarcastic glare, and then I disappear into the bathroom and close the door behind me. And the first thing I do is smell my hair. It does kind of stink. *Dang ferret.* I turn on the shower and shimmy out of my bathrobe. Then, I slip behind the shower curtain and wash off with my new body soap. It kind of smells like dryer sheets. Hannah bought it. She loves buying me things; I never complain. I lather shampoo into my hair next and then conditioner, and then I lather myself with the soap again—just to make sure there's no leftover ferret perfume on me. And when I'm done, I step out of the shower, towel off, throw on my robe again and twist my hair into another towel.

"Amsel," I call out to him as I open the door.

Steam pours out of the little room.

"Hmm?" he asks.

"I picked you up some soda. It's in the fridge."

"Oh, thanks, A," he says.

I hear him get up, and then I hear the refrigerator door open.

I, meanwhile, wipe the mirror with my hand. My reflection is distorted and blurry. I stare at it for a second. I feel as if I look young, but sometimes, I don't feel so young. I grab some lotion and massage it into my face before I scurry back to my room and throw on some old sweats.

On my way back to the living room, I drape the towel over the towel rack in the bathroom and run my fingers through my damp hair a couple times.

Amsel's sitting on the couch taking a big swig out of the can of soda when I walk in. I notice the ring on his finger against the red aluminum, and instantly, I suck in a quick breath. It's a gentle reminder that he's moved on and I haven't.

"You know that stuff's not good for your teeth," I say, plopping down onto the couch next to him.

He looks at the can in his hand.

"Then why do you always buy it for me?"

I narrow one eye at him and push my lips to one side. "I guess that does kind of make me your codependent."

"My what?" He starts to laugh.

"Your crutch."

"Well, crutch," he says, raising his can. "You smell much better."

I laugh and then shove his shoulder. He moves away from me but still manages to steady the soda and keep all the liquid inside the can. Then after he recovers, his dark brown eyes meet mine. And all of a sudden, there's a sobering look on his face.

"I heard you brought someone home," he says.

I don't say anything until I see a faint smile lingering on his lips.

"Well, word still does travel fast around these parts, doesn't it?" I ask.

He sits back and smiles liberally. "As fast as always," he confirms.

I make sure to keep an eye on him. "It doesn't bother you?" I ask, gingerly.

I wait for his eyes to find mine again. They do in the next second.

"Ada, what we had lasted but a moment and ended so long ago," he says with a straight, slightly sad face.

I just stare at him with a vacant expression until he starts to crack another smile.

Then, I shove his shoulder again and press my back against the couch.

"I'm just kidding, Ada," he says, laughing. "Well, sort of," he adds.

I shoot him a sarcastic glare.

"Ada," he says and then stops.

My sarcastic eyes quickly turn soft as I notice the change in his voice.

He takes a second and stares at the coffee table before he looks back up at me.

"Do you remember when we were kids and we used to play in that old barn on your grandpa's farm?"

I start to smile. *Only every other memory.*

"Of course," I say, simply, nodding my head.

"Remember that day when that big storm rolled through, and all of a sudden, it was lightning and thundering and pouring rain and we were stuck in that hayloft until it passed us?"

"Yeah," I softly say.

He looks into my eyes. "I was scared, but you weren't."

"I remember." My voice is almost a whisper as I lower my eyes. I remember the wind and how it howled through the alley below us. "But I really was scared," I confess.

He smiles. "Well, you didn't seem like it that day. You held my hand. That was the first time I ever fell in love."

The sincerity in his voice makes my heart swell.

"You broke my heart, Logan." His eyes falter and fall to the leather in the couch. "Ada," he corrects, lifting his gentle gaze again.

He tries to smile, and I do too before I scoot closer to him and wrap my arms around him. And a moment later, I feel his hands come to rest on my back.

"I love you," I whisper near his ear, holding him tight.

I feel his chest rise as he takes in a deep breath.

"I love you too, Logan," he exhales, not even bothering to correct himself.

Chapter Twenty-Nine

Sunday

"You wanna come with me, Ada Bear?"

Jorgen's throwing a little stress ball up into the air, catching it and then throwing it back up again.

"Where?" I ask.

"To the gas station. To get the M&M's."

I let go of a smile. "Sure."

I watch him throw the ball up one more time and then set it onto the coffee table.

"Okay. Let's go."

"Now?" I ask.

"Sure." He stands up and stretches his arms to the ceiling. "Why not?"

"All right," I say, giggling to myself.

I love days like this—like Sunday—when we can do things like go to the gas station just to get M&M's.

I find my keys, follow him out the door and lock it behind me. When I turn back around, he's holding out his hand. And as if it's second nature, I place my hand in his, and we head down the stairs together.

"So, you always go to the same gas station?"

"Yep," he says. "At different times though—depending on when or if I work that day."

I nod my head, and then we walk in comfortable silence for a minute. It's a beautiful, warm day. It's cooler than average, so it's not hot. The sun is out. There's a breeze. It's pretty much perfect.

"You look pretty," he says, suddenly breaking my thoughts.

I look up at him. I want to ask if I look different somehow from any other day, but I don't because the way he says it sounds so pure—as if there's nothing more to it than simply: *You look pretty.*

"Thanks," I say and then force my eyes to the ground at our feet. I'm sure I'm blushing.

I feel him squeeze my hand, and then I find his eyes again. He's smiling, and it makes me smile wider as we continue down the sidewalk—the same sidewalk that I've walked more times than I can count since I first moved here. It leads from the apartment complex to a little café called The Coffee Cup. I like to sit on the café's patio when it's nice outside and write sometimes. And then, about another hundred yards or so after The Coffee Cup is the gas station, nestled at the corner of an intersection. You wouldn't even know it was a gas station really if you didn't look closely enough. It's only two pumps outside a tiny, brick building with a clock tower shooting right out of its center. It looks more like a train station than a gas station.

But along the path to the café and the little gas station, there are big trees that hang over the sidewalk, shading us from all civilization. It's quiet, peaceful, relaxing.

"What was the Shakespeare quote?"

I look up at Jorgen.

"What?" I ask.

"You said that you decided to be a writer while staring at a quote by Shakespeare."

"Oh," I say and then pause.

"There is nothing either good or bad, but thinking makes it so," I recite.

"Hmm," he says. He seems to be thinking.

"Kinda like, life is what we make of it?" he asks.

I mull it over and then shrug my shoulders.

"Yeah, I guess," I say.

"You think that's true?" he asks.

I slowly bob my head. "Yeah, for the most part. I mean, we decide to frown or to smile—even when it hurts sometimes."

He tilts his face in my direction and narrows his eyes. "You know, I learn something new about you every day, Ada Cross."

I lower my gaze and laugh softly to myself. "And what did you just learn about me today? Do I want to know?"

He nods. "I learned that you just might be wise beyond your years."

I laugh out loud this time. "I'm not, I promise," I assure him. "I've only stolen those words. I didn't make them up."

"But you believe them," he says.

I know my face turns a little sad.

"Believe me," I say, "it's a work in progress."

Jorgen squeezes my hand, and all of a sudden, I notice we're at the door to the gas station. He holds it open for me, and I walk inside.

"It must be Sunday," the cashier immediately shouts over the counter.

Jorgen looks up, smiles and nods.

"M&M day," Jorgen confirms to the man.

The casual, ordinary way Jorgen responds to the guy behind the counter makes me laugh to myself. Here's this attractive guy—tan, muscular, tantalizing blue eyes, the whole bit—and yet he says things like *M&M day*.

I watch him dart into the candy aisle like clockwork and then go straight to the M&M's. And I just follow him and think about Hannah. And I think about her philosophy about there being a moment when you just know—like really know—you love someone. I think this is that moment.

He picks up a bag and then gestures toward the rows and rows of chocolate candy. "Do you want anything else?"

I shake my head. "It's M&M day."

He just smiles his crooked, sexy grin at me and then makes his way to the cashier and pays for the candy.

"See you next Sunday," the man says, waving his hand at us.

Jorgen tips his baseball cap at the cashier and then holds the door for me again.

"So, we can't eat the green ones?" I ask once we're outside.

He shakes his head and hands me the M&M's. "Nope, can't eat those."

I open the bag and pull out a green one and then throw it back into the bag.

"Does she actually eat these?"

He shrugs his shoulders. "I think so."

"I hope she doesn't mind us touching all of them."

"They've got a shell on them; it's okay," he says, taking the bag from my hand.

I laugh and scrunch up my brow. "What?"

He just looks at me.

"She doesn't care," he assures me, as he picks out a red one and pops it into his mouth. "She ate a grasshopper once. It had dirt on it."

My wide eyes rush to his. I watch him pour out a handful of the candies and then corral the green ones back into the bag. Then, finally, he looks up and seems to notice my questioning stare.

"I dared her to," he explains. "But I can assure you that these are cleaner than that grasshopper." He holds a single green M&M in between two fingers.

I try to stifle my laugh. "How old were you guys?"

"She was nine, I think. I would have been...eleven."

"That's awful, Jorgen."

"What? It was good protein for her."

I shake my head and grab the bag from his hand.

"Okay," I say, "so we eat all the colors but green and then..."

"And then we go home, tape the bag back up and put it in a little box and then mail it tomorrow," he says, proudly.

I feel my shoulders rock forward.

"What?" he asks.

"Nothing," I say, shaking my head.

"I thought you said it was..." He stops and seems to think about it. "*Cute*, I think was the word."

"I said strange but cute."

He shrugs his shoulders, but his goofy grin doesn't fade as he confiscates the bag again.

If I didn't know better, I'd swear I had always known this man and his silly grin. I had no idea that the day I invited him into my little apartment with his little pizza box in hand that I'd be inviting him into my life—for good. I mean, I don't know what happens after today or even the next day; I've learned that lesson the hard way. But I do know that no matter what happens, this man has forever changed me. It hasn't even been six months and he's wiggled his way into my heart and has stamped in permanent marker his name right there on the surface. And all the while, I just can't get over the fact that he's got this familiar way about him that makes me feel as if I've already lived an entire life by his side—as if we'd already experienced life's best joys, its most mundane moments and its saddest days and made it through them all, together—and for a moment, I almost wonder if we have. The thought makes me smile.

"Want the last one?"

I look up. He's got an orange M&M pressed between his fingers.

I open my mouth, and he places the M&M on my tongue.

"Now, we've got one bag of green M&M's." He proudly holds the bag out in front of us. He's wearing the same face he wore in that old photo with his first catfish. He's definitely a grown man now—no one would argue that—complete with stubble and a strong, square jaw and dark features—all but his eyes. But somehow, just somehow, he's managed to keep that same childlike expression that all but warms your heart and makes him so dang irresistible, all at the same time. And the best part is that I don't even think he knows just how irresistible he can be.

I snatch up the bag, and immediately, I feel my smile widen. "To Connecticut they go," I cheer, raising the green M&M's high into the air.

Chapter Thirty

The Message

"Jorgen."

Jorgen's phone beeps again, and I send it flying toward him.

"Message," I say.

He stops rubbing my feet to catch the phone with both hands. I watch him focus on the screen and read over the words. Then, I notice his eyebrows lift a little before he looks back up at me.

"What?"

"Oh, it's nothing," he says.

I shoot him a disbelieving look.

"It's just Kevin. He says he remembers where he's seen you."

"Oh," I say. "Where?"

He doesn't answer me at first. His eyes are back on the phone's screen.

"What?" he asks, sounding distracted.

I just stare at him.

"Where has he seen me?" I ask again.

"Oh. He didn't say."

His eyes fall from the screen and onto me before he sets the phone down onto the side table and presses his fingers into my feet a little bit more.

"Moberly's not too far from here," he says. "He probably had a crush on you when he was younger or something stupid like that, knowing Kevin. And I'm sure there's a long, dramatic, drawn-out story that goes with it too."

He looks back up at me, then scoots closer to me on the couch, puts his arm around my shoulders and kisses me softly.

"You want something to drink?" he asks, after our kiss breaks.

"Uh, sure," I say.

He pushes up from the couch and makes his way into the kitchen. My eyes travel to the television, but my mind travels back to the message. I glance up into the kitchen. Jorgen is searching in the refrigerator. I look at the phone, then back at the television and then back at Jorgen. He's still looking inside the fridge. I think about it for a second and almost hesitate before curiosity claims me and I lunge toward his phone and then quickly press the message icon. I feel a little like a stalker right about now. I mean, we share pretty much everything now—even our food and cars sometimes—so I trust him, but there's something else in that message that he isn't telling me.

Instantly, the screen lights up, and the message comes into plain view. I quickly force my eyes over the last sentence of the text: *I need to talk to you about her. ASAP.*

"Found it," I hear Jorgen say from the kitchen.

I quickly set the phone back down onto the table and slide back to my side of the couch.

"It was all the way in the back," he says.

I look up at him and catch him holding out the glass pitcher.

"Good," I say, forcing a smile.

I watch him turn away from me again and start pouring our drinks. *As Soon As Possible?* My heart is racing. My thoughts are in overdrive, and all of a sudden, Jorgen is standing over me.

"Your tea, sweetheart." He holds out a glass.

Sweetheart. He has never called me *sweetheart* before. The word kind of sticks to me in a way that feels strangely comforting, almost familiar. It almost kind of warms me somehow.

"Thank you," I say.

I watch him sit down and take a swig from his glass. He's in a tee shirt with *Truman Hospital* stretched across his chest in white letters. It's a fitted shirt; though, I'm not so sure it would be fitted on just anyone. And it's humid today, so his hair is extra curly, and his cheeks are a little sunburned, just like mine. We spent the rest of Sunday outside riding his bike and stopping at parks. *God, I never thought I'd ever say that again.* Though, I guess there are a lot of things I never thought I would say again, much less do. There were a lot of things, until this curly-haired, sunburned former football-player-slash-farm-boy came into my life and stole my heart without me looking.

"You know I love you, right?" I ask him.

I watch his gaze slowly travel back toward me before he rests his eyes in mine and then nods his head.

"You know I love you too, right?" he asks.

I lower my eyes before I meet his gentle stare again.

"Mm hmm," I say.

His smile widens. "What are you doing all the way over there?" he asks, waving me toward him. "Get your cute butt over here."

I shoot him a playful smirk. Then, I collide gently into his side and feel his muscular arm wrap tightly around me.

I feel safe here in his arms, and it makes my heart happy because the truth is that it's been a long time since I've felt safe in the arms of someone I could call mine.

Chapter Thirty-One

The Ring

"Hey," I say, setting my bag onto the wooden slats of the patio.

It's beautiful outside. There's a cool breeze in the air, but the sun is warm—a sign autumn will soon be here. I'm convinced that early afternoons like this were made for having coffee on The Coffee Cup patio.

"I got you your drink," Amsel says, eyeing a cup of coffee sitting on the table. "Extra cream. It's already in there."

"Thanks," I say, shooting him a happy smile.

"Well, it's not every day I get to steal you away—and on a Sunday," he adds.

He lets go of a wide grin, and it seems to take over the handsome features on his face. I get lost in it for a moment, remembering a different time, before I sit down and reach for the drink.

"How was your week?" I ask, taking a sip.

"Great, actually. We landed another client Wednesday."

My eyebrows instinctively lift. "Anyone I know?"

"Probably."

I start to smile again.

"Federhoffer's Deli," he says, before I even have a chance to guess.

"Wow! So, I can expect them to go national soon?"

"Honey, I can only hope," he says, flashing me another wide grin.

I just watch him for a second then. The way his smile is so clever, as if it holds a million thoughts; the way his starry eyes light up; and even the way he seems to always be so confident, it's so familiar, so comforting.

"I'm really proud of you," I say.

I set my cup down and rest my hand on his.

He stops and finds my eyes. There's still a smile hanging on his lips, but now it's more of a knowing smile—one that understands.

"I know we were just kids back then, but the moment I met you, I knew you were a fighter—like you'd always make it through anything that life threw at you," I say.

He laughs. "I had to be."

I lower my eyes and softly smile. "True," I say, eventually lifting my gaze to his again.

He holds his stare in mine for a little longer before he speaks.

"But no kidding?" he asks.

"No, really," I assure him, nodding my head. "I always believed you were a fighter."

"Really? Because I've always thought that about you, Logan—Ada," he quickly corrects.

My smile fades a little but ultimately stays.

"It's fine," I say. "I don't mind the name so much coming from you."

He squeezes my hand before I notice his gaze fall to my ring finger.

"The ring," he says.

I'm not sure if his statement is a question or just an observation. I pretend it's a question, though.

"I wear it sometimes," I say softly, lowering my eyes. "That doesn't make me crazy, does it?"

After a moment, I slowly lift my gaze to his and catch him shaking his head.

"Deep down, we're all some kind of crazy, Ada."

I laugh to myself. "Good answer."

He laughs too, but then the soothing hitches in his voice start to fade, and his familiar eyes spear mine.

"Someday, you won't feel the need to wear it anymore," he says.

I let go of a soft sigh. "It's still hard sometimes to imagine a day like that," I admit, looking at him now through hooded eyes.

I feel his hand squeeze mine a little tighter.

"Ada?"

Suddenly, there's a familiar voice cutting through our conversation, and immediately, it stops me cold.

My breath catches, and I look up to see a man holding a bag of M&M's. And behind him, I can see the little gas station sign, glaring at me. And then it hits me—it's Sunday.

I'm frozen. I watch Jorgen's eyes fall to my hand, cradled in Amsel's. And in plain sight, is the ring on my finger.

"I think we've met before," Jorgen says, turning his attention to Amsel.

I quickly take back my hand from Amsel.

"Jorgen," I manage to get out. "This is Amsel. He's... uh..."

I stop. I can't say it. I just can't get the words out.

Jorgen glances at me and then looks back at Amsel. "Jorgen," he says, extending his hand.

Amsel looks slightly confused, but he offers his hand and forces a smile nonetheless. Jorgen, however, doesn't even make an effort to smile.

"I'm Ada's next door neighbor," Jorgen says.

I cringe on the inside by the reference. I'm more than his next door neighbor.

"Oh," Amsel says, nodding his head.

It seems as though it just clicks for Amsel. His eyes widen and then quickly snap back to mine.

I try to smile, but there are too many thoughts running together in my mind. Jorgen's here, and Amsel's here, and I'm wearing a wedding ring, and two seconds ago, my hand was in Amsel's. I don't even know where to begin.

"I'll...uh," Amsel starts. His eyes trail back to Jorgen. "I'll just call you later. Okay, Logan?"

I manage a nod. And then, Amsel's gone.

I close my eyes. I want to open them and realize that this was all a dream—one big, awful nightmare. I feel the tears building. I try to push them back. I have to be a big girl. I have to face this. I have to finally face this.

I open my eyes to Jorgen's blue gaze. He hasn't moved an inch, and now his piercing stare is leaving a trail of hurt in my own.

"Jorgen," I start to explain. "I know what this must look like."

He's shaking his head, and I don't think I can fight back the tears anymore.

"Who are you...Logan?"

His words—my own name—hit my ears so coldly.

I close my eyes again to try and force back the tears. Then, suddenly, I feel him brush past me, and I quickly open my eyes and turn to see him walking swiftly away.

"Jorgen," I call after him.

He doesn't even slow down.

Fear courses through my veins until I'm literally shaking as my next thought battles to the forefront of my mind and my heart slams hard against my chest.

I know it's time. It's time to tell him everything— everything I've been too afraid to face, everything I've been too afraid to say, everything I've been too afraid to let go of. He deserves more than only half of me. He deserves to know all of me.

Chapter Thirty-Two

Secrets

I knock on his door and wait a couple seconds.

"Jorgen."

I knock again. I know he's here. His truck and his bike are still in the parking lot, and anyway, it didn't take me that long to grab my stuff and run after him.

"Jorgen, we need to talk."

I wait another minute, but still he doesn't come to the door.

"I'm sorry," I say, into the wooden frame.

I wait there for a few more agonizing moments.

"Jorgen," I plead one last time.

After another minute, I sadly realize he's not coming to the door. So I quickly venture back into my apartment and grab an index card and a pen. I go back to Jorgen's door, scribble the words *I love you* onto the card and then slide it in between the frame and the door until it sticks.

I step back then and stare at the little piece of paper with my honest words written on it. I might not have any other words together, but I do have those.

And a few more heartbeats later, I find myself slowly turning and inching my way back into my apartment. But I only make it to the couch before I just collapse and fall straight into the leather. All of a sudden, I feel weak and scared, as if I'm on the verge of losing everything—again. My eyes travel to a blank spot on the wall and fall quickly into a trance. I love Jorgen. I might be in love with another man—or the ghost of one—as well, but I love Jorgen. I love him with everything I am. In such a short time, he's become my world. And he's helped me to live again—to get back on the bike again, to do things I never thought I would ever do again. I can't imagine life without him. But it's also just hard to let go—so hard.

Suddenly, there's a knock at the door. The few thuds make me jump. I sit up and force my eyes to the sound. And within the next second, I'm jumping up and running over to it. I don't even bother looking through the peep hole before I throw the door open.

"Jorgen," I exhale when I see him.

He doesn't say anything. He just steps past me and plants his feet in the middle of my living room floor.

"Tell me it's not what it looks like," he demands flatly.

I slowly shake my head. "It's not."

His expression doesn't change.

"Will you sit with me?" I ask in a timid voice. "I'll explain everything."

I watch his chest rise and then fall. Then, he looks at the couch, takes a step toward it and sits down.

I try to smile, but smiling just doesn't seem right. So instead, I just make my way over to the couch and sit next to him.

"Jorgen," I say and then stop.

I take a deep breath and then force a steady stream of air over my dry lips. Somehow I know once I say it all, it will all finally be real.

I clear my throat and swallow hard.

"I was married."

His blue eyes rush to mine.

"Was?" he questions.

I pause and bite my bottom lip.

"The guy I saw you with," he starts. "He's the same guy. He's been here before."

He stops and turns his face away from me. I can see his jaw tighten.

"God, am I really that stupid?" he asks, rubbing his temples with his fingers, then balling his hands into fists. "You have this whole, other life, and I was too blind to see it."

It takes a second for it all to click.

"Amsel?" I ask.

He looks at me, and his eyes seem eerily cold now.

"Yeah, whatever his name is," he says, turning his face away from me again.

"Jorgen, it's not at all what you think."

His head snaps back toward me.

"Really, Ada? Because it looks pretty damn bad."

I lower my eyes and gather up my courage.

"Amsel is James—James Amsel," I say. "He's my husband's brother. He was...is my husband's brother. He's...he's Andrew's brother."

Everything just stumbles out of my mouth. I've never had to explain who James is. I've never even had to explain who Andrew was. And now, I can't seem to get the words out and put it all in the right tense. I look up at Jorgen. He seems to be processing everything.

"I just need a minute," he states, standing up.

I close my eyes and take a breath. When I open my eyes, he's staring at my hand.

"I just need some time, Ada," he says, as he makes his way to the door.

His words come out so soft, almost broken.

I look down at my hand and the ring still on my finger.

"Jorgen," I call out after him.

I try to say more before he escapes back into the hallway, but I can't. I can't say it all to his back. I can't say everything I need to say to him as he's walking away.

I stop and feel the tears freely cascading down my cheeks as I realize that even if he had stopped—even if he had stopped and turned around—I'm not so sure I would have had the courage to say: *My husband left me, but not on his own time.*

Chapter Thirty-Three

The Nightmare

"**Y**our helmet, Wife." He hands me the pink helmet.

"Thank you, Husband."

I take the helmet and squeeze it over my head.

"Husband," I say again, just to feel it on my tongue.

I hear the click of the helmet's strap under my chin and watch as Andrew slides the marriage license and the camera inside the backpack and zips it closed.

"Guard this with your life," he says, angling back toward me.

I force my arms through the bag until it's resting on my back.

"Oh, and I put my sweatshirt in there too just in case you get cold on the way back," he says. "Let me know if we need to stop, so you can put it on."

I nod my head, and the big, pink helmet moves with it.

"I love you, Logan Amsel. Forever and a day." He reaches back and squeezes my leg.

I adjust the backpack, then tighten my arms around his waist. "I love you too, Andrew Amsel."

There's a moment, and then suddenly, the purr of the bike's engine fills the air around us. The sound grows louder and louder as the bike leaves the curb in one swift motion, forcing my body backward. I squeeze my arms tighter around Andrew's waist.

"Forever and a day," I whisper, pressing my cheek against his shoulder.

It's early afternoon. Wednesday. June 10. The sun is shining. There are cotton-ball clouds in the sky, and I can see the open road ahead of us. The warm air is hitting my arms and brushing past my bare shoulders. It feels good against my skin. We take a turn, and I hold on to Andrew tighter and move with his body. I have so much love for the boy I'm holding. I caress the ring on my left hand with my thumb and think about the perfect life we're going to have together. I'm thinking about our little house in the country, our three, little scraggly children we're going to raise together and all the places we're going to go when something happens and the dreams all shatter.

My weight shifts forward, and the bike turns sharply. There's something big with fur running to the side— maybe a deer. I hold on to Andrew as tightly as I can. Then I see the pole, and I brace myself for the impact.

It feels as if it's only been a matter of seconds and I'm waking up in a ditch on the side of the road. I'm on my back, and all I can see is blue sky. I tilt my head to the side, and my head aches. There are wildflowers growing up everywhere all around me. And there's a smell of burnt rubber in the air. It gets stuck in my throat and makes me cough. I swallow hard and try to take shallower breaths.

"Andrew," I whisper.

I'm terrified. I want to find him, but I don't want to say his name loud enough and he not answer me back.

"Andrew," I whisper again.

I hear the sirens of police or ambulances or something.

I turn on my side and sit up. The backpack is still on my back. I pull its straps across my chest until they're touching, remembering Andrew's warning. And then my head starts spinning. I force my eyes closed for a second. And when I open them, I notice that there's a gash on my leg. It's bleeding, but it doesn't look too bad. I look toward the highway. The sirens are getting closer.

"Andrew," I say a little louder.

I unsnap my helmet and pull it off. It falls to the ground, and I quickly push up onto my feet. But suddenly, my head spins out of control and just as quickly, the earth is pulling me back down again. I fight it, though, and manage to get back to my feet. And in the next moment, my eyes frantically go to searching the tall weeds around me.

"Andrew," I yell this time.

I spot him several yards away. He's on his back. He's not moving. He's not moving! I panic and lose the moments. Somehow, the next thing I remember is shaking Andrew's shoulders and calling out his name, while someone else is pulling me off of him. I hold onto

226

Andrew's shirt as tightly as I can. I don't want to let him go.

"Please," I scream. "No."

There are more of them now, pulling on me. I try to fight them off, but I lose.

I don't know how much time has passed when I wake up on a stretcher in an ambulance, and the first thing I notice is that the backpack is gone. Where did it go? I take a deep breath and exhale every piece of joy in my soul. And immediately, the tears start streaming down my cheeks. And I cry, and I cry, until I just stop. I just stop crying.

"What is your name?" I hear the man beside me ask.

It's not the first time he has asked me, but it is the first time I have actually heard it as a question.

"What's your name, sweetheart?" he asks again.

My eyes lift and I notice the bright shade of blue in the man's eyes. Then, my gaze falls onto a silver pin the man is wearing on his shirt. I focus on it. It's shiny. So shiny. I watch the man take the pin from near his collar and put it into my bloody hand. There's so much blood. I don't even know if it's all mine.

"Your name," he says again.

"Mrs. Amsel," I whisper, still staring at the pin, now in my hand.

The warm liquid floods my eyes again, and I quickly force my eyelids shut. I caress the metal pin's edges with my fingers inside the palm of my hand. I'm starting to feel numb. My whole body is starting to feel numb. I press one of the pin's edges into my hand until I feel a sharp pain. Then, I take a deep breath and slowly force the air back through my lips.

My alarm is blaring some song from the top hits station on the radio. It's so loud, it sounds like it's right next to me. I lift my head and notice I'm still on the couch. Then immediately, I feel the sting of a night full of my lingering memories.

I force myself to sit up. The light is on above me, and the blinds are wide open, but on the other side of the patio doors, it's dark. I take a second to rub my eyes before I slowly push myself up and stagger toward the song playing in my bedroom. When I get close enough, I throw my hand on top of the alarm, and instantly, the room grows silent again. I glance at the clock. There's a big, bright green six on it. The little, mesmerizing glow in the dark room captures my full attention for a few seconds, until I snap out of it and fall onto the edge of my bed. Moments pass, and I just sit there and stare at the beige wall in front of me, trying to convince myself that someday the nightmare won't haunt me. And then, suddenly, I remember Jorgen.

Chapter Thirty-Four

Name

I don't even bother changing out of the clothes I wore yesterday—the same clothes I fell asleep in. I charge to my door, push past it and plant my feet on Jorgen's welcome mat.

I take a second to rally my courage. Then, I knock three times on the hard wood. A few moments disappear before I hear rustling on the other side. And all of a sudden, the knob turns and the door opens. He's still wearing his jeans from yesterday, but his shirt is gone. I notice his abs and the muscles in his chest right before I charge into his apartment.

"What time is it?" he asks, rubbing his eyes.

"It doesn't matter," I say. "We're talking about this."

I hear him suck in a breath.

"Okay," he concedes softly, turning away.

I watch him close the door and take a seat on one of his barstools, but I don't sit down. I just stand.

"Jorgen."

I wait until his eyes meet mine. And when they do, I continue.

"I was married. I was eighteen. It was right after graduation."

I stop and try to gather some more courage to say the words that I've needed to say for a long time now.

"We had known each other since we were kids," I go on. "He asked, and I said *yes*. I had dreamed about it since I was nine. I didn't even have to think about it. Our parents didn't know—until they found the marriage license after..."

Jorgen's voice stops me.

"Ada, why don't you go by your first name?"

I think my eyebrows instinctively collide. He sounds so calm now—as if he's not mad anymore. But I don't understand his question or maybe I just don't understand why he's asking it.

There's dead silence for a long, agonizing minute. Then, I look into his eyes.

"I couldn't...," I start. "The last thing he—Andrew, my husband—said to me was my name and the words: *I love you* and *forever*. I couldn't hear my name and not think of those words anymore."

I try my hardest to fight back the tears.

"See," I go on slowly, "we were on his bike, on our way home from getting married, and we didn't make it home...he didn't make it home."

I watch Jorgen's face grow pale, and it breaks my heart. I wish I knew what he was thinking.

"But Jorgen, that was a long time ago, and I..."

"Ada," he says softly, stopping me again.

There's a word on his lips, but nothing comes out. He finds my eyes, stays in them only a moment and then quickly sends his gaze to the floor.

"Ada, I was there that day."

I think I stop breathing for a second.

"I couldn't find an ID on you. You said your name was Mrs. Amsel." His eyes lock in mine. "And you were looking at my pin of St. Michael, so I took it off, and I gave it to you. You still have the pin. It's on your shelf."

My heart is racing now. I'm trying with everything in me to calm it and to think—to just think, to put it all in order.

He looks down at the floor and then back up at me.

I don't believe it. It can't be. I would have known. I would have remembered. I would have remembered...

His eyes...

I look into Jorgen's blue eyes, and then it hits me. Why didn't I see it before?

Tears start to blurry my vision. I'm shaking my head. Images from that day, images of Andrew, images of the paramedic—Jorgen—are racing through my mind, and I feel as if I can't breathe again. I feel as if my two lives are colliding and they shouldn't be.

"I started to put it all together last night." He shakes his head. "I mean I should have figured it all out before. Hell, I might have known it all along and just didn't want to believe it—didn't want to believe that you had suffered that much or that I had seen you suffer that much. I don't know."

There's silence then. He doesn't break it and neither do I for long, sad moments. I'm aware of every heartbeat in my chest. I'm conscious of every breath that passes over my lips and every blink of my eye. I'm consumed by the acts of purely living. I barely notice him get up and walk toward me. And suddenly, I feel his arms surrounding me, drawing me closer to him.

"Ada," I hear him say, "I'm sorry. I should have listened to you yesterday."

The tears are flooding my cheeks now. I try to respond, but the words just come out only as sobby resemblances of words instead.

"Ada, it's okay," he says, gently stroking my hair.

He was there. He was there. I repeat the little sentence over and over in my mind.

"Ada, I remembered your face, but I couldn't, didn't want to place it," he whispers in a shaky voice.

I feel a gasp instinctively escape my lips.

He was there. He knows everything. He knew everything this whole time. Only until now, I guess, everything he had known was connected to some other life—some other face that wasn't mine.

"Kevin was working with me that afternoon," he continues, as if he's remembering it all for the first time.

I take a second and swallow the lump in my throat.

"He remembered me," I say, through my tears.

I feel his head nod above me.

"I never talked to him about it, but that must have been what he wanted to tell me," he says.

I try to control the sobs and wipe away the tears.

"Jorgen," I manage to get out. I pull away from him and find his eyes. "You have to know that I love you. I don't want to live in my past anymore. I want to live in my present—with you. I don't want to lose you."

I lay my head against his chest again, and then I feel his arms squeeze tightly around me.

"I love you too, Ada," I hear him whisper. "I'm yours. I'm not going anywhere, sweetheart."

Sweetheart. At his last word, the world falls away, and I feel my heart exploding—exploding with not only love for this man but appreciation for giving this tortured soul a second chance—a second life.

"I love you," I say again, with everything I have left in me. "I love you so much."

Chapter Thirty-Five

The Grave

I go to the spot that's etched into my memory—at the end, near the corner. There's a big oak tree that sits on the other side of the fence. It shades the spot, and it seems only fitting. But when I see the piece of stone jetting up from the earth, I stop cold and just stare at it. I don't know what else to do. Of anything I've ever done in my life, even more so than starting over in a tomorrow without him, this makes me the most terrified. That stone might as well be a ghost.

I stare at it a little longer. I don't want to look at it, but I force myself to. It still doesn't seem right that his name should be there, etched in rock under the words, *Loving husband, son and brother.* And it doesn't seem right that there's not much time between those two numbers. Eighteen years. Only eighteen, short, beautiful years. And I think about that little dash that separates those two years, and it's hard to believe that our life fit into that little space—that all our moments, all our dreams, all our joys, all our laughter, all our tears and all our smiles are held within that little dash. I push back the warm tears as I try to rationalize it. It's just not possible.

I force myself to walk closer to the stone. It feels like the frost-covered ground is more like wet concrete as my feet, little by little, struggle to take each step. But finally, I reach it, and I slowly kneel down so that I'm at eye level with the carved words. I glance at the dark gray indentions, then quickly turn away and stare at the frozen grass instead as my heart slams hard against my chest. Half of me is saying I can't do this; I'm not strong enough. The other half says I must. So after a moment, I force my eyes back, and suddenly, I feel my hand moving toward the stone, and soon, my fingers are pressing against the indented letters that make up the word *husband*.

I've been here once—the day I said goodbye to him for the last time. But I've never seen the gray stone that bears his name. I finish moving my fingertips over the word, and then I follow the letters in his name, until my eyes fall to a spot below the dates where there's an inscription. I had requested it be there, but I hadn't thought about it since then until now. In small letters is the little quote that he might not have gone a day without saying: *There is nothing either good or bad, but thinking makes it so.* I wanted it there because the quote is Andrew, because it says what he would say if he could. It says: *Don't cry for me.* And now, everyone who passes by here—everyone who never had the chance to meet him—will know who he was.

The quote makes me smile, but it also forces another tear down my cheek. I wipe it away with the back of my hand and focus on another inscription below the quote. I run my fingertips over each letter in the words: *Forever and a day.* And when I get to the last letter, my head falls to my knees, and I try to control my heart as it grows ever heavy in my chest. He wrote the words in a tree; I had to make sure they were written in stone. And I had said those words that day—that last day with him—but I had whispered them, and I don't think he could have heard me over the bike's engine. I have replayed that moment in my head probably a million times now, but each time now, when I say the words, I shout them. I make sure he hears them.

I feel like sobbing, but I don't. Instead, I sniffle, swallow the hurt in my throat and wipe my eyes again.

"Andrew," I whisper.

I watch my breath freeze in the air, and I try to force back the flood of tears that I soon realize I can't possibly stop from streaming down my cheeks. It's been years since I've said his name out loud—as if he were right in front of me.

"You weren't supposed to leave me," I whisper.

I pause and force my lips up, but the smile quickly fades away.

"If I would have known that day was going to be our last day together, I would have held you tighter. I would have kissed you longer."

I wipe my eyes with the back of my hand and just sit there in silence for a moment. I stare at the last inscription. I try not to look at the name above it.

"I've met someone," I whisper, at last. "He's not as crazy as you."

I laugh to myself and sniffle some more.

"But he's just as amazing," I say, and then I try to smile again through my tears. "You would have liked him."

I swallow hard, and I just sit there in silence for a while—thinking, letting the hum of the quiet carry me away. I think about our first kiss behind that big hay bale in that dusty hayloft. I think about the way his muscles moved in his arm as he carved our love into that old oak tree. And I think about the way my name looked as if it belonged etched in that black ink onto his heart. And then I remember the look in his eyes when he told me he liked my sundress on our wedding day, and I replay that last, perfect smile that he ever gave me. Then, I take a rock out of one coat pocket and a piece of torn paper from the other. And I allow my eyes to follow over the words on the little page one final time:

September 2, 2000

Dear Diary,

I really hate being the new girl. I hope Daddy never gets another promotion. I never want to move again. I miss my old school, and I miss my friends. But I guess it's not all bad. Sara Thomas showed me how to do a backflip on the monkey bars today, and she pretty much never left my side. I'm pretty sure she's going to be my new best friend. And don't tell anyone, but there's also this boy in my class, and he lives just up the road, and he's so, so cute. He acts like he doesn't like me, but I don't think he's a very good actor. I'm going to marry him one day.

I hold the page torn right out of my old diary tightly in my hand. Then, I place it on the ground near the base of the stone, and on top of it, I gently set the rock that, once upon a time, penned our love into eternity.

"I love you, Andrew," I whisper. "I'll love you forever...and a day."

I softly kiss the inside of my fingers and then press them to the hard, cold stone. Then, I take another second and wipe the tears from my eyes before I slowly stand up, inhale a breath of cool air and walk away.

Chapter Thirty-Six

Six Months Later

Once the words were said, somehow, it had made it all real. And I can't help but notice that Jorgen had been the only one who had made me want to make it all real—to pull off the Band-Aid and start to heal. I wanted to heal for him.

I take the marriage license from Hannah and lay it into the cardboard box. Then, she hands me Andrew's championship ring, and I catch its blue jewel sparkling in the light from the open window. *My something blue.* I always kept it in a little shoebox tucked away inside my closet. I take the championship ring now and the little diamond wedding ring, and I put them together into a small ring box and then lay the little box next to the marriage license.

"Here, this too," Hannah says, handing me a little, metal pin.

I shake my head and take the pin. "No, that can stay out," I say. "That's actually my fiancé's."

Hannah just smiles back at me.

"Well, then, I think we've got everything," she announces.

"Hey," I hear a familiar voice call out from the other room.

"We're in here," I say.

I stretch a piece of packing tape over the top of the box.

"What about your name?" Hannah asks.

I stop running my hand over the tape and look up at her.

"I've been Ada for so long now. I don't even know what it's like to be Logan anymore."

I think the truth is that I feel more alive being Ada and maybe also that Logan is in some way my last piece of Andrew. And there's still a tiny piece of me that wants to leave him something.

Jorgen is standing in the doorway now. I meet his eyes, and I think he reads my mind.

"I've only known you as Ada," Jorgen says. "I've always loved Ada."

I slowly let go of a smile before I look back at my sister. "I'm Ada, Hannah."

Hannah seems to understand because she gives me her look of approval.

Amsel comes in then and Jorgen pats him on the shoulder.

"Ada," another voice calls out from the other room. "I've brought a lot of hands to help you move."

The voice comes from a petite, very pregnant brunette who squeezes into the room and plants her feet in front of Amsel. Amsel puts his arm around her and kisses her on the lips.

"Thanks, Erin," I say.

"We'll have you all moved out and in your new home in no time," she says, eyeing up Jorgen.

Jorgen finds my eyes, and a crooked smile dances to life on his face.

God, I love him.

"Red?"

I open my mouth, and he sets an M&M onto my tongue.

"Mmm," I say. "Red tastes good."

He laughs and pours more of the candies into his hand.

"Green."

"Put it back," I say.

I stretch my leg to where the metal links of the porch swing connect, and with my bare toes, I play with the delicate, little chains. The house is quiet now. Everyone's gone home. Boxes are scattered in every room. There are even a few, which didn't quite make it into the house, stacked up next to us. I turn my head in Jorgen's lap and look out onto the field in front of us. There's a summer breeze gently pushing the wildflowers and the tall grasses back and forth. It almost looks as if the grass is waving. I smile and turn onto my side and nuzzle back into Jorgen's lap.

Off to the left, there's a narrow, white-graveled driveway. It starts close and meanders to a line of apple trees, then disappears. The sky is a beautiful mix of blue and pink watercolors fading into each other at the base of the tree line. It looks more like a painting than real life. That's my view from this porch swing—simple, untouched, exactly how I always saw it. There's a lot to do to make this little patch of earth a home, but I can't wait to make it a home with Jorgen.

I feel his hand come down and gently brush a piece of my hair back from my face.

"What are you thinking about, Ada Bear?"

His voice is soft and thoughtful.

"About our little house in the country," I say.

I turn onto my back again and stare up into his beautiful sky-blue eyes.

"You know, I always saw it this way," I go on. "I saw the tall grass and the apple trees and the long, gravel driveway. I saw it all from this porch swing. And when I looked up into the eyes of the man I was resting in..."

I stop and start to smile.

"I saw your face," I say. "I know now it was you all along."

Epilogue

There is nothing either good or bad, but thinking makes it so.

I still think about that quote from time to time. And I think maybe I was supposed to live two lives. Maybe I was supposed to meet two wonderful people and share my life with them. Maybe Shakespeare and Andrew had it right. Maybe the story of our life is what we make of it. I mean, we're dealt the rain and the sun, but maybe it's up to us to push away the clouds in order to see the rainbow.

My story began with Andrew Amsel. It began on the playground at Cedar Elementary and on our childhood adventures along with Hannah and James at my grandpa's farm. It began in the hallways of Truman High and under the stars at Jenson's slab. My life began in those little moments with that starry-eyed dreamer who stole my first *I love you*. And it still stings sometimes thinking about the story that Andrew and I could have had—the one we spent hours of our summer nights in the bed of his truck and under that old oak tree scheming and dreaming about. I'm convinced that that first heartbreak will never truly go away, and yet I don't know what my story would have been like without Jorgen showing up across the hall in the next chapter either. I can't even picture it. Andrew was my first love. Jorgen is my true love. I think I was meant to find them both—to give each one of them a part of my heart.

I still love Andrew very much. I gave him a piece of my heart a long time ago, and once you give that away, I've learned you don't so easily get it back. Though, I'm not looking to get it back either. I'm concentrating on today now—on just those precious moments that are right in front of me.

"Mommy, I found a ring."

I look down at my little girl. Her little pigtails are like sprouts shooting out of her little head.

"You did?" I ask her. "Let me see it."

She proudly presents me with her tiny hand. I glance at the ring now wrapped around two of her little fingers, and my smile fades.

"Whose ring is it, Mommy?"

I take a second before I answer her.

"It's mommy's ring, sweetheart."

She stares at the ring for a moment.

"Where did you get it?"

Her little voice is so curious. I try to force a smile.

"A boy," I answer her.

She's dangling the ring now from her little finger.

"From Daddy?" she asks.

I look at her little, perfect face that seems to be completely engulfed in the ring and in the mystery behind it, and then I pull her closer to me and take the ring into my own hand.

"No, sweetheart, it was from Mommy's first love."

I kiss the top of her head.

"Someday, you'll have a first love too," I say.

She's quiet for a moment. I know she's thinking.

"Why isn't Daddy your first love?" her little voice asks then.

The hint of a smile starts to edge up my face.

"Because Daddy is my true love, darling," I say to her.

She fixes her eyes on the ring in my hand again. I can tell she's soaking up my words, but I'm not sure if she knows what they all mean.

"What if I just want one?" she eventually asks.

I push out a soft laugh.

"I pray that your first love is your true love, sweetheart."

She turns to me and presses her little, delicate hand against my chest.

"Mommy?"

"Yes, dear?"

"Does your heart hurt?"

My smile falters a little. I have no idea how this little person can sense so much feeling.

"No, sweetheart," I say, shaking my head. "Mommy's really happy. She's really happy she had the chance to hold everyone she held in this life—especially you."

I wrap my arms around her and squeeze her little body tightly against mine. And I hold her for a little longer than I usually do before I take a deep breath and let out a gentle sigh.

"Okay, sweetie, time for bed."

I let her go, and she climbs into her bed as I stand up and pull the covers over her.

"Okay, what burrito am I making tonight?" I ask her.

I watch her eyes shift to the ceiling as she pushes her lips to one side and places a single finger on her chin.

"Cheese," she eventually screams.

"Just cheese?"

"Just cheese," she confirms, with another shout. "Cheese," she cheers again.

"Okay, okay, a cheese burrito it is."

I bend down and tuck the blanket in all around her. I'm not sure how this little bedtime ritual started exactly, but she loves it.

"Making my cheese burrito," I sing. "Gotta make it really tight."

I tighten the blanket around her a little more, and then I stand up and look at the outline of her precious, little body under the covers.

"I think it's ready now," I say. "Time for prayers."

"Let me start, Mommy," she pleads.

I nod my head. "Go ahead."

She carefully pulls her arms out from under the blanket that's now molded around her and meticulously interlocks her little fingers and closes her eyes.

I watch her. Then, I take a seat on the bed next to her and close my eyes as she starts her prayer.

"Dear God, thank you for Rover. And for my bestest friend Charlotte's dog, Max. And please help that dog that me and Daddy saw yesterday at the animal doctor. Please help his leg to get better."

Laura Miller

She stops, and I open my eyes and find her eyelids still tightly closed and her little fingers still interlocked.

"And God," she continues, "please bless Mommy and Daddy and the boy who gave Mommy the ring."

My heart melts at her little words, and I start to smile again as I wait for her pretty blue eyes to open. They do a few seconds later, and then her little smile devours her face.

"And thank you, God," I start, and she joins in immediately, and we both say it together: "For all you have given, for all you have taken away and for all you have left."

She smiles again when we finish, and her eyes instantly travel to the other side of the room.

"Daddy!"

I look up and find Jorgen standing in the doorway. He laughs at our little, excited girl, and then he meets my stare.

"Hey, babe," he says.

I shoot him a smile, and for a second, I'm caught in his perfect blue eyes. I swear I'll never be immune to them.

"And how's my little peanut?" he asks, making his way toward the bed.

He bends down and tickles her. She squirms and giggles until his fingers stop gently raking her sides.

"Daddy?" she asks, after she has calmed down again.

"Yes, dear?"

"Is Mommy *your* true love?"

Jorgen looks at me. I only shrug my shoulders and smile.

"Honey, Mommy's my only love."

I can see the corners of his mouth slowly turning up, and I get lost in him again. I love him for the man that he is and the woman he makes me. If Andrew taught me how to love, Jorgen taught me how to love again. He taught me how to smile again, how to laugh again, how to give my heart again. I love him. I love everything about him, even his crooked smile. He's perfect, and he's as sexy as the day I saw him with his shirt off through the peep hole in my little apartment with Hannah. His muscles are still nearly the size of Hannah's thighs, and his eyes are still the most unique shade of blue I've ever come across. He's in his navy work pants and white shirt. And near his collar, there's a pin of Saint Michael.

My smile widens as he takes my hand and cradles it in his. But my eyes are still drawn to the shiny, silver pin. That same pin of Saint Michael was my hope when all hope seemed lost—that little nudge pushing me onward, assuring me that I would make it, promising me that I would feel again. But little did I know that afternoon, amongst the blood and the tears and the chaos, that my hope wasn't the pin—but the man who gave it to me.